I0737266

# my heart's desire

A YAKUZA PATH ROMANCE

## AMY TASUKADA

*My Heart's Desire* (A Yakuza Path Romance)
© 2022 Amy Tasukada

All rights reserved.

No parts of this publication may be reproduced, stored in a retrieval system, or transmitted in any form or by any means, electronic, mechanical, photocopying, recording, or otherwise, without the prior written permission of the copyright owner.

This is a work of fiction. Any similarity between the characters and situations within its pages and places or persons, living or dead, is unintentional and co-incidental.

ISBN ebook : 978-1-948361-34-7
ISBN Paper: 978-1-948361-35-4
Cover Design: Natasha Snow
Outline Critique: M.S. Wordsmith
Line Editing: Susie Selva
Copy Editing: Lyss Em
Formatting: Champagne Book Design

**Some high school romances just won't fade.**

As a high-ranking yakuza, Yuuki enjoys his relatively quiet job. If only his mother would stop asking for grandchildren. Unwilling to come out, he contemplates a sham marriage just to shut her up. After all, it's not as if he'll ever be lucky in love again.

Blacklisted after his divorce, the only reason luxury suit designer Kazuki is still in business is his yakuza clientele. Desperate to find new clients, he starts looking for a collaborator for the upcoming fashion show. But who's daring enough to partner up with him?

When Kazuki's high school sweetheart walks into his shop, all those worries disappear. Although Yuuki has far from forgiven Kazuki for his past betrayal, Kazuki wants nothing more than to rekindle their love. But then he learns Yuuki is in the yakuza…

Can these two mend their love, or are they now too different to thread their lives together?

**Buy *My Heart's Desire* to find out if they were always meant to be!**

# acknowledgments

Thank you to my family, without whose support this book would not be possible. To Nell Iris, who is not only the queen of fluffy romance books, but also a dear friend. Addison, thank you, too, for your comments and help. Leigh Hart, thanks for being my go-to plague buddy and your wonderful plotting ideas. Thank you to my Patrons, whose support I can never thank enough.

Finally, you. Thank you for giving my book a try.

my heart's
desire

# chapter 1



*September 12*

A part of Yuuki knew he'd regret it.

One day, there would be no need to worry about the obligatory cake to celebrate another year he lingered on earth or if his smile appeared sincere. One day, his birthday would come and go like a flickering flame. One day, his mother would die, and he could forget the banal celebration of his birth.

"It feels like only yesterday you sat at this table, and I helped you with your homework. You'd get so mad when I pointed out a mistake." Mother's voice sounded teetering and light like a gust of wind stole its strength. "Thirty-five already. I can hardly believe it."

"You say the same thing every year," Yuuki mumbled.

If she heard, she pretended she didn't.

For as long as he could remember, they'd celebrated his birthday at the round table, too big for the apartment. The table's wooden veneer was a better indication of the years gone by than the number of candles on Yuuki's cake. From the chip in the center where six-year-old Yuuki had accidentally dropped a flower vase—they hadn't had flowers since—to the collection of light scratches where thirteen-year-old Yuuki had decided to give the family Pomeranian a lion cut, to the dent along the table's spindle legs where Yuuki spent most of last year nervously kicking while his mother vomited in the bathroom.

She sipped her mimosa and let her fingers tap against the glass. Prominent veins scarred her crumpled crepe-paper skin. No expensive creams could undo the years of back-of-house restaurant work made worse by last year's medical scare. The treatments had turned her coal-black hair gray, when it wasn't falling out, and clouded her sharp eyes under a layer of memory lapses and fog.

In Yuuki's youth, people would say he and his mother looked alike with the same eyes and high cheekbones. Not exactly the thing a young boy wanted to hear, but as he grew older, Yuuki didn't mind.

Yuuki leaned over to scratch the ear of one of the five Pomeranians Mother had collected over the years. "I would get upset because you'd give me the answers to the homework. I wanted to figure it out myself."

Mother laughed. "That's right, but after a few years, I couldn't help you at all. You were always such a bright kid. All those hard classes and cram school on top of it."

Yuuki had thought academic excellence would produce his dream future.

It hadn't.

It never could.

If Mother hadn't been so spineless, she could've told him sooner. Instead, the heart-to-heart about Yuuki's limited opportunities had fallen to his aunt.

"Aren't you going to eat any cake?" Mother asked.

"The lunch you made was so delicious. I don't think I have any room left."

"But it's *your* birthday cake. Eat a slice, for me, at least."

Obligation set in, and Yuuki cut into the cake, vanilla with sugar-glazed mandarins on top. His favorite. He slid the thin slice onto his plate and took a few bites. A bit too sweet for his liking, but Mother always cared more about looks than substance.

"It's good," he said because not saying it would be rude.

"I bought it from that little bakery you liked."

Yuuki had no idea what his mother was talking about, but he nodded along like a good son. He'd stopped counting the number of mismatched memories his mother attributed to him.

"Now it's time for your present!" she said.

"You didn't need to get me a gift."

"What kind of a mother would I be if I didn't give my son a gift on his birthday?"

She pulled out a little blue box with a white ribbon attached. Yuuki's shoulders tightened, catching the ecstatic gleam in her eyes.

"Go ahead and open it!"

Maybe she'd finally gotten the hint and inside would be a tie and a pair of socks. He could always hope.

He plastered on a smile and slid his finger underneath the paper seam. He folded the paper back on itself and took in a breath when he opened the box. Inside was a green onesie with a yellow duck embroidered on the chest.

"It'll be perfect for my grandchild," Mother said.

Yuuki didn't have a girlfriend.

Yuuki *never* had a girlfriend.

Mother continued. "I think this is going to be your year.

You're going to meet the woman of your dreams. Last year, it was too hectic for you to look, but this year will be different."

Not that he wanted a girlfriend. A boyfriend? Sure, but that relationship wouldn't result in the grandchildren his mom had been aggressively hinting at more and more for the past six years.

He wasn't about to tell her he was gay. There were some subjects he never wanted to discuss with her, and his sexuality was one of them.

The white Pomeranian sitting in the chair beside Mother barked.

"See? Even Peaches is excited to have a grandchild she can play with," she said.

Then a chorus of yippy barks joined. Not from Peaches but the rest of the Pomeranian pack waiting at attention on the floor. Five dogs in total, each with its own saccharine-sounding name.

"Shush." Yuuki patted Lucky's head. "I have to find a woman first, so don't get too excited."

"Have you tried one of those dating apps? All the ladies at mah-jongg said it worked wonders for their children."

"I don't know."

"It's not like there're a lot of women in your line of work. Most people are meeting others through apps first. There's nothing to be ashamed of."

Yuuki rubbed his neck. "Dating is hard to fit into my schedule."

Her eyes narrowed. "Didn't you get a promotion? Miko told me it would mean less work for you."

"Everything is still new, so lots of things are in the air. Aunt Miko isn't on the ground level anymore. So she doesn't know about the day-to-day."

"You're a handsome guy. You should have no trouble finding a wife."

"Usually, you have to date a while before you get married."

"I want to hold my grandchild before I die."

Yuuki winced. "Don't say that. You've been in remission for a year now. You're not going to die anytime soon."

"You said yourself you have to date this woman first. How many years is it going to take before the proposal? You've promised you'd try for years now."

Her eyes glistened, threatening tears. If Yuuki had been stabbed, it would've hurt less.

She'd sat at the same table and cried the day his father had left them. Yuuki had still been in grade school, and when he'd opened the front door, her tears broke him. He'd vowed that day to never make her cry.

Yuuki gulped, but the lump in his throat stayed. "I'll look into the app."

She rubbed her eyes. "I'll ask the ladies what ones their children used when I see them later tonight."

"I'm sure they're all the same."

"You want the ones for people who are serious about finding someone to marry. There are so many out there. I want to make sure you're on the right one."

"Maybe there's a dating app for mothers looking on behalf of their children."

"I've searched. There isn't."

"I should've known," Yuuki said.

"I can set up the account for you if you're busy with work, or I could even message some girls that look like good daughters-in-law," she suggested.

"I want a specific type of woman, so it's best if I look."

"Are you telling me I've waited all these years because you're picky?"

"You want the perfect daughter-in-law, and I have to make sure she loves dogs, right?" Yuuki stood and grabbed dog treats from the kitchen cabinet. The pack of dogs ran after him. "Have you taught any of them any new tricks?"

"Not yet. Maybe rolling over could be next."

"Maybe something useful like how to make dinner."

Mother laughed. Yuuki could finally swallow the lump in his throat. He squatted and had each of the dogs shake his hand before giving it a treat. Yuuki glanced at the clock.

"I need to get going to work," he said.

"You didn't take off on your birthday?" Mother asked. "You're working too hard. That's why I don't have a daughter-in-law."

"I promise to look into those dating apps."

"You'd better! Don't forget your gift."

Yuuki grabbed the box, hugged his mother goodbye, and headed for the train station. The onesie became trash, but the residue of his mother's words couldn't be tossed aside so easily.

On the gay forums he frequented, he'd seen a section for people requesting marriage-of-convenience arrangements. Maybe he could post there and find a woman who had children, but then he'd have to deal with the children. Maybe he could find someone with an older teenager.

Yuuki closed his eyes and leaned back in the train seat. The soft sway and the calming feminine voice announcing each stop made it easy to forget the urgent tone in his mother's voice. Yuuki would think about it later. Given his line of work, no one would be excited to have him as a partner, fake or real.

He stepped off the train.

The summer turf war with the Korean Mafia had left most of the old yakuza guard dead. Yuuki was lucky to still be breathing, let alone promoted. The only constant in the chaos was the weekly trek to pick up his boss's dry cleaning.

With the clothes slung over his back, Yuuki walked the rest of the way to an old building.

Without the usual Kyoto yakuza crest, the office building looked like any other, and it had been hidden beneath enough shell companies that no detective could uncover the true owner. Yuuki punched in the building's security code and opened the door of the side entrance. Light poured into the dimly lit room thick with cigarette smoke.

"Hurry up!" Jun cursed under his breath and moved the ice pack to cover his eyes.

Yuuki stepped inside, the door slamming shut behind him.

"And don't be so loud."

"Sorry." Yuuki put away the dry cleaning, trying not to disturb his hungover boss. Not that Yuuki could blame Jun for last night's bender.

The newest Kyoto mafia don, Father Murata, blurred the line between passionate leader and psychopath. Yesterday, Jun had his first meeting with the boss. Yuuki had waited downstairs, and even *his* ears still rang from the tongue-lashing Jun had received.

"I can come back later," Yuuki whispered.

"No, stay." Jun's voice cracked and shook as if he were in the midst of his own personal torture. "Eventually, these meds will kick in."

Jun took off the ice pack and rubbed his head. His rounded face and plump cheeks gave him such young features that he looked more like a kid playing dress-up in his father's suit than a yakuza in his late thirties. Jun tapped out a cigarette from his pack, and Yuuki rushed to light it.

"What's the status of that thing you were working on for the clubs?" Jun's dark glare glowed amber with the cast-off light of the cigarette.

"The subscription feature?" Yuuki asked. "We talked about it a few weeks back."

"That! You said it could generate me more money. How?"

"Yes, still in the building phase, but if we pushed through a subscription model where people pay a flat fee for unlimited entry to your clubs, you could be making a huge profit because everyone ends up forgetting about it like they do gym memberships. I can set up a fee directly for processing the credit cards and really rake it in using the same methods we use for the brothels."

Instead of patrolling the streets, Yuuki's new job had been following Jun around like the Pomeranians did with his mother. Unlike with his mother and the dogs, Jun usually got bored of Yuuki after dinner and sent him home. Even when his required workdays were short, boredom set in for Yuuki, and he'd quickly devised ways to use his passion for programming.

"Good," Jun said, though Yuuki doubted he understood any of it. "Keep what you're doing between us."

"Of course."

They sat in silence while Jun puffed away on his cigarette and rubbed his head. The same moments as always, waiting for Jun to decide what obligations mixed with his own side hustles needed his presence that day.

Jun smashed the spent stick in the ashtray. "I need a new suit."

"I can pick one up at your—"

"Not anymore." Jun slammed his fist on the desk, then winced. "That bastard Murata has a thing against foreign brands."

"Oh."

"Murata believes all the nationalistic bullshit his father spewed, so that means no more foreign suits. Not if we want him on our side. I'm not going to end up like Ikida, in jail for something no one else disapproved of."

Yuuki nodded. "We should begin going to all the local festivals. From what I hear, Father Murata goes to each of them."

"Suggestions like that are why I made you secretary." Jun glanced at Yuuki with a glint of approval. It was the first positive thing Jun had said that day. "We should get going. I set up an appointment at Okamoto Bespoke Suits. It's the place Murata shops."

Yuuki raised a brow. He'd known someone in high school with that family name. But Okamoto was a common name. They couldn't be the Kazuki Okamoto Yuuki knew.

Heat flooded through Yuuki's body, and a tingly ache pressed against his chest.

No, that Okamoto was better left as an annoying memory.

# *chapter 2*

Even with Kazuki's office door closed, the hum of the sewing machine backstitched into the room. The hum meant business. It meant he could neglect the paperwork on his desk, knowing there'd be enough money in the bank to pay for everything. A year ago, it wouldn't have been the case.

Kazuki tossed out the steeped tea leaves and grabbed the mug. He squeezed between his cluttered desk and the extra bolts of fabric blocking half the kitchenette counter and headed to the workroom. He dropped off the green tea at Shizuri's workstation. Her precision behind the machine fortified Kazuki's business.

"Thanks." She reached for the mug without missing a stitch.

"Tell me if there's anything else I can get you."

Kazuki waited, shifting his feet between the echoes of silent longing for something else to scratch his urge to please. She never spoke. She never glanced up from the machine.

"I'll get back to cutting the suit," he said.

The cutting table dominated the length of the workroom.

When he wasn't working, he needed to fold the table up for Shizuri to walk around without turning sideways. The cozy space had been perfect for their past dribble of customers, but with the typhoon of new clients, they were barely treading water. Even while Kazuki drowned, he still took each customer's order, pushing their completion dates further and further into the future. He'd lost sight of the shore months ago, and the only thing he could do to survive was swim.

He rolled out a bolt of silk-wool blend, a stunning mixture of threads of octopus-ink black and ebony. The deep hues conjured an unparalleled ominous aura, one fitting for its owner. Kazuki laid out the paper pattern on the fabric and traced the lines with triangle chalk.

Through the lines and curves, time slipped. The long strands of Kazuki's hip-length hair fell over his shoulder. He'd intended to cut it three years ago when he'd opened the shop, but there had always been something distracting him. With each centimeter his hair grew, the more he liked the deliciously dark length. He tied his hair back, took up the fabric shears, and cut.

A sharp sting shot through his finger. "Damn," Kazuki hissed, shoving the nicked finger into his mouth.

The hum of the machine stopped. "Did you get any blood on the fabric?"

"Not that I can see," Kazuki mumbled, the metallic taste coating his tongue.

Shizuri pulled out the first aid kit. "It won't be the last time that suit will taste blood."

The soon-to-be suit belonged to Mr. Murata, the newest Kyoto mafia don. When the young yakuza had strolled into the store, Kazuki hadn't known the client's devious profession. Since then, every customer swaggered in with the arrogant pride of a yakuza.

"It's almost lunchtime already." Kazuki wrapped a bandage around his finger. "Have you decided what we should get for lunch?"

Shizuri shook her head, the flipped-out strands of her pixie haircut remaining perfectly in imperfect place. "Mr. Murata's fitting is tomorrow, and I still have to hand baste the pieces together after you're finished bleeding on them."

"But you haven't left your sewing machine all day. You deserve a full lunch."

"And who is going to sew all these orders?"

"I'll help."

"And get blood all over the other pieces too?" Shizuri laughed. "Though with our current client list, the blood wouldn't be a big deal."

"You're exaggerating."

"Am I? Have you looked at the client list lately? I'm working on a suit for the only non-yakuza client for at least five months." The truth in her pointed tone hurt.

Kazuki's gaze lingered on the fabric, and his stomach twisted. He took up the scissors and returned to cutting. "It can't be that bad."

He couldn't imagine working with anyone other than Shizuri, but her bluntness still caught him off guard. She'd been trained in a notable luxury shop but was supposedly ostracized when she couldn't bite her tongue at every jab management took. Her skill had kept her employed until they'd learned she dated women. Kazuki couldn't have cared less, as he dated both men and women, and since then, she'd worked at his shop.

The door separating the workshop from the store opened. Fujio staggered inside, his face pale and his hands shaking.

"It's one of them a-again," he said, his voice cracking.

*Them.*

Yakuza.

Fujio's good looks matched his smooth conversational skills. It had made him perfect for explaining the suit-making process to clients while taking their measurements. He'd been hired a few months ago so Kazuki could stay in the back and tackle the mountain of unfinished orders. Yet anytime a yakuza walked in, Fujio could barely speak, let alone hold a measuring tape. Mobsters left even Kazuki uneasy, so he couldn't blame Fujio for his fear.

Kazuki should've put a block of time aside to teach Fujio how to finish buttonholes and pockets. The time-intensive task was easy to pick up, and Fujio could do it when he staggered into the back because of yakuza… once he could steady his hands.

"I'll deal with the customers," Kazuki said. "Did you ask what they wanted to drink?"

Fujio rubbed his hands together. "W-whiskey for them both."

Shizuri laughed. "Those yakuza are getting bolder with each order. Do we even have any whiskey?"

"We got a bottle as a thank-you the other week."

Kazuki pushed open the swinging door to his office and pretended the pile of paperwork wasn't on his desk. He dug through the alcohol cabinet until he found the bottle and put together an elegant tray. He headed out of the office/kitchenette/extra fabric storage room and stopped in front of Fujio, who was still pale.

"Why don't you take lunch early today?" Kazuki suggested.

Fujio could only nod.

With the tray in hand, Kazuki headed to the front of the store.

Wooden floors covered the showroom. It wasn't the

largest shop, but it had enough space for a sitting area with a few leather chairs and a pedestal for easier measurements.

"I humbly apologize for the delay. My name is Kazuki Okamoto. I'm the owner of the store, and…" His words dried up in his throat the moment his gaze locked with Yuuki's.

Seventeen years ago, Kazuki had gotten lost in Yuuki's enchanting honey-and-amber-colored eyes just as he did today. Kazuki's heart longed to reach out and connect like it had at their first student council meeting.

The years had changed Yuuki. He'd ditched the glasses and added about three suit sizes worth of muscles. Even with the muscle, Yuuki couldn't be a yakuza. No one had spent more time studying in high school than him. Kazuki had often daydreamed about what adult Yuuki would be like and had always imagined him cooped up in the dark, staring at a computer screen with his glasses halfway down his nose.

Yuuki must've just happened to have walked in with the yakuza, and Fujio had been too shaken up to check.

Kazuki cleared his throat and continued, "We make the world's finest bespoke suits and are the only company to use exclusively Japanese fabrics and trims. Whatever style or look you desire, we can accommodate."

Yuuki rolled his eyes while the younger-looking man tapped on the arm of the leather chair. Even with his youthful face, the aura around him screamed danger.

Kazuki placed the tray on the end table beside the two and grabbed the client chart by the changing room. When he turned back, Yuuki had opened the whiskey bottle and poured a glass for the other man.

Kazuki swallowed. Yuuki was a yakuza.

"I'm Jun, and this is my associate Yuuki." A sly smile crossed Jun's face as he squeezed Yuuki's shoulder. "How does this process work? I've only had semicustom suits made before."

"Today, we'll get your measurements and pick a style and fabric. At our first fitting, the suit will be loosely sewn together for easy adjustment to give you the perfect fit. Then you'll come back for your final fitting. If all goes well, that will be your last, but we can continue to have as many fittings as necessary until you are happy."

"Easy enough." Jun sipped his whiskey. "How long does it take?"

"We have a large waiting list, so our current time is five to six months out. I'll take your measurements today, and then we can talk about suit designs and fabric selection. Who would like to go first?"

Jun took off his coat and stepped onto the pedestal. His current clothes looked forced into place with none of the ease that came with a custom-made suit. Kazuki measured Jun's neck first, stealing a glance at Yuuki, but he seemed more interested in his whiskey than recognizing his old boyfriend.

"Did you catch the Tigers game?" Kazuki asked while he measured. "They're really hot this season. Maybe they'll make it to the championship."

Yuuki loved baseball, but he didn't even perk up at the mention of his favorite team. Jun didn't care either, giving Kazuki a grunt for an answer.

"I see you're more of a whiskey guy." Kazuki chuckled. "What did you think of the Yamazaki?"

That got Jun talking.

Kazuki knew next to nothing about whiskey, but that wasn't the point. Jun needed to be at ease and remember the experience as relaxing, like visiting a longtime friend. Kazuki asked a few more opened-ended questions, but even with his brain screaming at him to pay attention to whatever whiskey brand Jun touted as the best, Kazuki's attention always fell back to Yuuki.

Would he taste of the same bundle of anticipation and nerves after all these years? Kazuki's fingers longed to reach out and touch him, wanting to explore each new contour of muscle and each orifice to compare them against his memories.

"Didn't you already take that measurement?" Jun asked.

"Double-checking. People usually relax more as it goes on, so those first few are sometimes a little different." Kazuki laughed. "Now we can start with the fun stuff. Let's look into fabric and finishings."

"You're familiar with Nao Murata?" The cutting edge to Jun's voice struck like a needle through Kazuki's nailbed.

"Mr. Murata is a valued customer."

"I want one of his."

Mr. Murata would no doubt kill Kazuki if he gave any one of his subordinates the exact same fabric. Jun would be fine with a similar color.

"We can easily achieve that feeling, but he has gotten a few different styles—"

"He must like one more than the others. Get the one he likes the most for me. Also, that six-month wait isn't going to work for me." Jun reached into his pocket and pulled out a stack of money as thick as Kazuki's thumb. He stuffed the cash into Kazuki's front breast pocket. "This should cover a rush order, correct?"

"We can make arrangements, of course."

The small pocket could barely hold the amount, so Kazuki stuffed it into his pants.

"That's what I thought." Jun snapped his fingers, grabbing Yuuki's attention. "You're next."

# chapter 3

Yuuki's stomach burned like an overclocked CPU. He didn't want to be in the same room as Kazuki let alone close enough for Kazuki to measure his inseam.

"Me?" Yuuki forced a chuckle, even as his stomach flamed.

"You're my secretary, and we both have to make Father Murata happy." Jun turned toward Kazuki. "Today's Yuuki's birthday. The suit is a surprise gift to him."

"You're being too generous. I don't need a new suit."

"You think I wanted a new one?" Jun pointed to the stage. "Now get up there."

Yuuki couldn't say no to a direct order.

He finished the whiskey left in his glass, then rubbed his hands against his slacks. Then his phone vibrated. A call. Yuuki smiled. Even a small delay was better than none. If he was lucky, it would be an emergency, and they would have to leave.

Yuuki fished the phone out of his pocket. Kurosawa's number flashed on the screen. He was the underboss for the syndicate, and his calling meant either Father Murata had decided to demand a meeting, or the Korean mob had attacked.

"This is Yuuki," he answered.

"Everything's fine." Kurosawa's cigarette-scarred voice came over the line. "I have business to discuss."

An attack would've been horrible, but at least they'd be rushing off to help. Instead, all Yuuki could do was hand the phone over to Jun. He snapped his fingers at Yuuki, motioning for him to get on the pedestal, then walked outside to take the call.

Yuuki pressed his lips together but followed the command. Kazuki's happy-go-lucky smile couldn't look dumber. Yuuki held his breath and waited, hoping the tingling at the back of his throat would subside.

Kazuki had always had an innate ability to talk to anyone and make them feel at ease in a matter of minutes. It was what had won him the popularity contest for high school president and what had stolen Yuuki's teenage heart. But Yuuki wasn't seventeen anymore. He'd been able to ignore Kazuki as he'd schmoozed up Jun, and he could do it again.

But for the first time he could remember, Kazuki was silent. He did his job taking the measurements and nothing more.

His long face and angular jaw always had the girls fawning over him, but for Yuuki, it had been Kazuki's eyes that had ripped open the walls surrounding his heart. Kazuki's eyes were otherworldly nebulas of golden brown.

During their school years, Kazuki had always skirted the boys' hair length policy. Unrestricted by rules, it seemed Kazuki had allowed his luscious locks to tumble to his waist. Yuuki's fingers ached to reach out and get lost within Kazuki's hair again.

"Could you hold your arms out for me so I can measure your chest?" Kazuki's monotone cruelly gnawed away Yuuki's warm memories.

Yuuki held out his arms, and Kazuki measured. If only Kazuki would allow his fingers to press a little heavier so Yuuki could really feel the touch. He swallowed down the flicker of desire. Their relationship had ended a lifetime ago, and it wasn't like Kazuki had proved to even be friend material after what he'd done.

"You're still clumsy as ever." Yuuki nodded to Kazuki's bandaged finger.

"You do remember me!" Kazuki's charming smile slid into place like it had been punched out of Yuuki's memory. "All this time, I thought you'd forgotten me."

"How could I forget how much of a jerk you were?" The caustic tone surprised Yuuki, but no amount of wanton longing could erase what Kazuki had done.

"I told you about Hana because I wanted you to know the truth."

"I would've appreciated knowing you were engaged before we started dating."

"I told you the marriage had been arranged when I was twelve!" The wrinkles around Kazuki's eyes deepened. "I was a sexually confused bisexual kid. Of course I said yes when my dad offered me an easy way out instead of figuring out my feelings. My parents never brought it up again. I had completely forgotten when I started dating you. Then, during New Year's, they brought up helping arrange the wedding, and I called it off right away. It would've been wrong to not tell you as soon as I could."

Kazuki's words reopened the scar Yuuki had thought faded long ago.

"You told me when you did it so *you* wouldn't have the guilt weighing you down during our college entrance exams. Instead, I was stuck thinking about how much I hated my boyfriend while trying to use angle-sum identities. I spent three years in cram school for that day, and you ruined it!"

"Yuuki, I—"

"Sure, you told me you called off the marriage, but you couldn't keep it to yourself until after the college entrance exams? I bombed them because you only thought of your own feelings, which was why I broke up with you. Then you went ahead and married her a week after graduation!"

Memories exploded like a burning supernova. After the test, Kazuki had continued being the high school prince like nothing had happened, while Yuuki had spiraled into complete solitude. He'd been alone when he'd received the abysmal test score that even the lowest-ranking college wouldn't accept.

"I was a stupid kid." Kazuki gnawed on his lower lip. "I'm sorry."

"I don't care about your apology anymore."

Screaming in space would've done Kazuki better than uttering another word. Yuuki looked away but caught Kazuki's quivering lip in the mirror.

Yuuki thought he would've enjoyed seeing the pained expression on Kazuki's face, but instead, a pit the size of an asteroid lodged itself in Yuuki's stomach.

"The marriage didn't work out anyway." Kazuki's words were small and anguished. "We've been divorced for three years now. That's why I opened this shop."

"When I wrote that note about never wanting to talk to you again, I meant it. Now do your job." Yuuki's sharp tone pricked his ears.

The rest of the measurements were taken in silence, even the inseam gauged without any fanfare.

Kazuki transferred his notes to his clipboard. "You still wear boxers?"

"You flirted better in high school."

"It's necessary for the best fit."

Yuuki didn't remember Jun getting asked about underwear, but Yuuki had been too caught up in his own thoughts to know for sure.

"I switched to boxer briefs," Yuuki mumbled.

"Hmm, what color?"

Yuuki's eyes narrowed. "You can't possibly—"

The door opened, and Jun strolled back inside. "We've got a meeting."

Kazuki confirmed the phone numbers for both of them and thanked them for their business, his words nothing but hollow formality. If Jun had stayed, no doubt Kazuki would've kept his formal tone for the whole ordeal.

Despite their disaster of a conversation, the flames flickering in Yuuki's stomach warmed his heart. The long hair looked good on Kazuki, and Yuuki had never been more turned on by rolled-up sleeves in his life.

Yuuki brought the car around and opened the door for Jun.

"We're meeting Kurosawa at the usual place," Jun said.

Kurosawa's office was on the other side of town, though it always felt like Yuuki had to spend more time finding parking than driving there.

Having dropped off Jun, Yuuki punched the code into the keypad on the inconspicuous gray building himself. Yellow clung to the walls, both from age and cigarette stains. Most of the offices sat empty, but laughter poured out of Kurosawa's.

Cigarette smoke swirled between Jun and Kurosawa.

The Korean attacks had decimated all the high-ranking syndicate members. Kurosawa had been selected as underboss shortly after Jun's promotion. Combined, they had less than four months of experience in their new positions. Kurosawa had once had enough muscle that, even in his forties, he could take down the youngest recruit, but since becoming the underboss, his muscles were slowly turning into a rounded belly. Though, anyone would be stress-eating having to deal with the syndicate's new godfather.

"Did you get the suit?" Kurosawa asked.

Jun took a drag from his cigarette. "We were getting measured when you called. You really think something as simple as a suit will help?"

"Father Murata is unpredictable, but a Japanese-made suit will be something he'll expect from all of us."

"He's not one to be subtle, eh?"

"Especially with how much he loves the way his new secretary takes care of his morning wood."

Kurosawa and Jun broke into laughter.

The Kyoto godfather was gay. While no one would joke about his sexuality to his face, they did it behind his back. The older members were stuck in the past, but Kurosawa was the biggest homophobic bastard of them all. Jun never initiated the slurs, but he laughed along with them.

Yuuki was closeted, and he had no plans to come out. Still, knowing their godfather was unabashedly gay made Yuuki more at ease.

"Anyway, on to business. The Hokkaido prison decided to limit the number of phone calls Miko can have to one a month," Kurosawa said.

While everyone clamored to fulfill Father Murata's wishes, in reality, he only acted as interim syndicate leader until Miko was released in about five years. All major decisions required Miko's blessing. Since they were still on the heels of a turf war with the Korean mob, reducing communication to once a month forced them into a bad position.

"I heard the local mob has an in at the prison," Jun said.

"Yes, I think they're the ones who cut the cord in order to

force our hands and form an alliance. We need Miko's permission to start the process, but we already used the monthly call."

Kurosawa and Jun turned toward Yuuki.

His eyes widened. They'd never cared about him before, but then it clicked.

"And she's on strict family-only visitation," Yuuki said.

"Exactly," Kurosawa said.

"I'm the only one who could ask since she's my aunt."

"Exactly," Jun added.

These were the only times the family really needed him. He'd always hung around important people but simply followed orders.

Yuuki sat a little straighter. "When do we leave for Hokkaido?"

"As soon as possible. Jun will fly out with you to get the ball rolling once you get her okay," Kurosawa said.

Yuuki nodded. "I'll make arrangements to travel there right away."

Kurosawa looked toward Jun. "You've been gathering information on the Hokkaido syndicate?"

"Their biggest imports are drugs, prostitution, and lots of illegal porn," Jun said.

"The drugs are something we'll have to hide from Father Murata."

"I'll set up everything so all he'll have to do is drink sake."

"That's for the best."

Jun lit another cigarette, and the meeting continued with a discussion of the day-to-day health of the different wards.

Yuuki pulled out his personal phone and searched for flights. He needed to do laundry before they left or else he wouldn't have any underwear.

He swallowed. A flash of heat and nostalgic desire washed over him.

In high school, Kazuki and Yuuki had been in different classes. Notes between them would be stuffed into shoe lockers and passed off after their shared lunch. In one of the letters, Kazuki had asked about the color of Yuuki's underwear. Yuuki couldn't write boring blue and gray. So he'd written red, put it in Kazuki's locker, and bought a pair on the way home.

The next day, during lunch, Kazuki and Yuuki had snuck off to the quiet section of the school where they'd always eaten, but instead of opening up their bento boxes for lunch, Kazuki had tugged Yuuki into an empty bathroom stall. He'd asked to see the vibrant underwear, and Yuuki had obliged. Kazuki had gotten on his knees, and Yuuki had pushed his fingers into his hair. It had been long back then, but with it being waist-length now, Yuuki could twist it around his hand. Yuuki licked his lips.

"Yuuki. Yuuki," Jun called.

Yuuki shook his head. "Sorry. Looking up flight information."

"What day looks best?"

"The day after tomorrow." Yuuki's stomach grumbled. "Excuse me."

Jun laughed. "You hungry?"

"I can't believe it after the birthday lunch my mom made."

"It's about dinnertime. Let me take you out."

Yuuki's mouth opened, but no words came out. Eating dinner with Jun meant only one thing, and Yuuki would rather starve.

# chapter 4

Kazuki's fingers slipped, and the red highlighter bounced onto his office floor. He picked it up and glanced toward the small window by the kitchenette. The view wasn't much, just the air conditioner unit for the building, but it allowed for something of an escape. Instead of a glimmer of the sun, Kazuki was greeted by the darkness of night.

He picked up the highlighter and tried not to think about how much time had passed since the store closed. Especially since it looked like the only thing he'd done was add more paperwork to his desk.

He turned to the last page on his list of clients and highlighted Jun's and Yuuki's names. Then he turned to the beginning and counted the names marked in red, but so many took up one page that Kazuki stopped and counted the names *not* highlighted. He flipped through the pages until he got to the end.

Three.

Only three orders for the next six months weren't yakuza. Shizuri was right. Almost everyone who stepped into the store was a yakuza, even Yuuki. It was a far cry from the engineer Yuuki had dreamed of being, though Kazuki had wanted to be an astronomer.

Kazuki glanced back to the window and played with the ends of his hair. It had been years since he'd even thought about the stars let alone gone out and properly stargazed.

During the summer break of his senior year, Kazuki had convinced Yuuki to take a day off from cram school and go stargazing. They'd spent the afternoon on trains and buses until they'd ended up at a tiny village in the mountains.

Night hadn't helped with the humidity, and they'd stripped off their layers of clothes in a failed attempt to beat the heat. Naked and underneath the stars, they'd planned their future together. They'd both go to Tokyo University and rent an apartment together close to campus. Yuuki would find a job engineering the programs Kazuki would use to discover far-flung galaxies.

That day, everything had felt possible, but teenage dreams broke under the pressure of reality.

Kazuki brushed his hair over his shoulder and grabbed tomorrow's task sheets. He headed out of his office and placed Shizuri's list by her sewing machine. She glanced over at it while hand finishing the buttonholes on a vest.

Her sleek eyebrow rose. "Is this right? It says you want me to start Jun's suit tomorrow, but he only came in today for measurements."

"It's a rush order."

"They all want rush orders."

"This one came with a stack of cash this thick." Kazuki held up his fingers to simulate the amount.

Shizuri whistled. "With that much, you could hire a yaku-za-only front-of-store clerk."

"I can't blame Fujio." Kazuki rolled out the heavy paper

to translate Jun's measurements into a pattern. "Getting so close to yakuza can be scary."

"I showed him how to baste pieces together when he was back here."

"Did he like it?"

Shizuri shrugged. "Who cares? We had yakuza clients all day, and he was too much of a coward to even serve drinks. He had to do something or else you'd be paying him to drink tea and cower."

Kazuki rubbed his neck. "I'll talk to him tomorrow. Maybe he'll like helping you out better."

"The main question is, how soon will it be until our customers aren't gangsters?"

"It should be a temporary thing."

"Until we've outfitted every mobster in Kyoto?"

Kazuki laughed. "I hope not."

"And what if we mess up an order or we don't meet their expectations? We don't want the Kyoto mob angry at us. You saw those headlines about shops getting ransacked. I don't want to be worried about getting attacked while sewing."

"I don't think they would do that—"

"We could end up in the middle of their turf war without even knowing," Shizuri mumbled.

Kazuki pressed his lips together and concentrated on the pattern, wanting to avoid Shizuri's discerning gaze.

"I had to stop taking a paycheck to keep the doors open before," Kazuki finally said. "It's been nice not having to worry…"

Kazuki knew he had to do something, but it wasn't like he could hang a No Yakuza sign on his front door.

Shizuri snipped off the end of the thread. "Have you even started planning how to entice normal clients?"

Kazuki barely had time to think about what he was eating for dinner let alone a marketing campaign.

"It's getting late," Kazuki said. "Why don't you head out, and I'll finish those buttonholes?"

"And come in tomorrow to see you drooling on the nice wool again?"

Kazuki winced. If Shizuri were a boxer, she'd KO every opponent. "That only happened twice."

"More like a dozen. I'll stay for another two hours to get a head start on all these rush orders."

"At least let me buy you dinner," Kazuki said.

"That eel place. It's always good."

"We had eel yesterday."

"They have many different ways of preparing the eel. Today I want double fried."

Shizuri might've switched between the two most expensive things on the menu, but it was the least Kazuki could do. Especially with her overtime butting up against the legal limit. Kazuki needed to do something, but there was never any time to think of a way to please everyone. Kazuki rubbed his head. It wasn't worth worrying about today. Once things quieted down, he'd be able to focus.

"I'll call in the order, then pick it up," Kazuki said.

"Then get the ball rolling on hiring another tailor or two." She laughed. "We'll need them now but especially when you get the fabric ordered for the fashion show line."

Kazuki's eyes widened.

He hadn't thought of the Kyoto fashion show since he'd gotten accepted earlier in the year, but then more clients had come, and orders had piled up. His sketchbook lay hidden underneath the stacks of paperwork, tossed aside like old thread.

Five months to create a line would be a challenge. If Kazuki concentrated, he'd be able to pull something together.

Shizuri grinned. "You could always work with a collaborator if you haven't started."

If she weren't right about everything, Kazuki would've been angry.

"I've been working on designs," he said.

She shot him an I-know-you're-bluffing look.

Kazuki headed to his office, called in their order, and managed to find his sketchbook in the second stack of papers from where he'd thought it would be.

He tapped his pencil against the blank page. Usually at that point, he would daydream a bit, draw a few lines, and in an hour or so, end up with something. But today, instead of daydreaming of luxurious fabrics or high-class events for the person wearing the suit to attend, all Kazuki could think about was Yuuki.

How did someone like him end up in the yakuza?

It wouldn't be the first time his sketching had turned into what-is-Yuuki-doing-now curiosity. Kazuki had never gotten over his first love, but everyone had that problem.

He made a few lines on his page, but they resembled Yuuki's high cheekbones and the way his hair swept over his bright eyes.

Kazuki groaned at himself and rested his forehead on the page. He wasn't going to get anywhere thinking about Yuuki. Not with the show only five months away.

Maybe a collaboration would be better. It could help bring new clients into the shop. Kazuki booted up his laptop, located in the third stack of papers he'd thought it would be under, and pulled up his old contacts. He could come up with a well-written collaboration request before picking up dinner.

# chapter 5

Jun's and Yuuki's steps echoed against the polished marble floors. They were almost as impressive as the view from the penthouse hallway. Too bad Yuuki couldn't jump out the window and avoid the whole evening. He swallowed and hoped his unease didn't show on his face.

"She's been expecting us," Jun said.

Yuuki nodded, not trusting his voice to speak.

Jun raised his hand to knock on one of the scarlet doors, but it opened before his knuckles connected.

"Mother, you remember Yuuki." Jun's tone came out gracious, lacking the usual sharp edges.

Jun's mother kept her gray hair tied back in a low, tight bun. Her wide mouth and thin eyebrows didn't match Jun's rounded, childlike features. They barely resembled cousins let alone mother and son.

"My little swan, you've come home for dinner, and you brought a friend." She opened her arms.

They embraced, which Yuuki could understand, but then they kissed. Not on the cheek but on the lips. He clutched his stomach and glanced back to the hallway window. He'd seen countless men die before his eyes, yet he couldn't stomach the kiss.

"It's so nice to have you both." Her voice was artificially sweet like she rehearsed in the mirror each morning. "Come on inside. Dinner is almost finished."

They shuffled into the small entryway, switching shoes for slippers.

She stood in front of Yuuki, blocking his entry. "My little swan told me it is your birthday."

"That's right." Yuuki took a step back.

"You'll have to forgive me for not preparing a cake."

"I had lunch with my mother. She gave me enough cake for a week."

"How nice to hear my little swan keeps such good company. It's important for sons to visit their mothers."

Miss Kubo clasped her hands together. Her red, red, red nails were as sharp as daggers and shined with the viscera of the last victim who'd dared to disagree. *Unhinged* wouldn't begin to describe her type of madness.

Along with strictly referring to Jun as "my little swan," Miss Kubo had decorated the condo with hundreds of swan figurines. If that had been her only quirk, Yuuki would've thought it was cute, but against everything else, Yuuki was convinced during one visit she would smack him across his head with a crystal swan. He'd wake up dazed in a swan bathtub with her fist in his stomach, pulling out his intestines to make an origami swan.

She ushered them into the dining room and took a few minutes to finish dinner. They each received a chicken rice bowl with a cracked egg on top. Yuuki slowly unwrapped the swan-folded cloth napkin and watched Jun and his mother take a few bites before breaking his yolk—hopefully chicken and not swan—and mixing it with the rice. The feathered swan centerpiece stared back at him.

"How are the clubs doing?" she asked.

Jun easily talked with his mother. The conversation held none of the silent pauses and calculated answers Yuuki had to navigate with his own mother. Jun could easily rattle off events of the week between bites. More importantly, throughout the hour-long conversation, she never brought up how Jun needed to get married or how he didn't even have a girlfriend. Jun was three years older, and his mother should be triply aggressive about the topic.

"Don't you want grandchildren?" Yuuki blurted out.

His words hung in the air. Yuuki's muscles quivered.

"I'm sorry." Yuuki laughed and rubbed his neck. "My mom keeps pressuring me about finally getting some."

Miss Kubo smiled, her teeth poking out to touch her bottom lip. She put her hand over Jun's and squeezed.

"Jun's a man," she said. It was the first time Yuuki had heard her use her son's name. "He bought me this place. Why would I want a little boy?"

Miss Kubo took a sip of her wine. All the while, her sharp, toothy grin stayed on her face.

Yuuki cleared his throat. "Ah, yes, I see."

He couldn't eat another bite with the glare Jun shot him.

"Yuuki, how did you meet my little swan?" she asked. She always asked.

Still, Yuuki swallowed, not sure if the olive branch of conversation she offered was real or a trap.

"We worked in the same ward," Yuuki said.

"Oh, that's right. Wasn't there a fight or something?"

"A branch of the Korean mob attacked when Jun and I were making the rounds. They surrounded us. I froze, but

Jun kept it together and made sure we both made it out alive. Without him, I would be dead."

The first time Yuuki had told the story, he'd added more enthusiasm and flare, but now he ran through it like an order at a restaurant.

"Isn't that something?" She smiled at Jun. "Such a man, putting others before his own safety."

Yuuki was certain Miss Kubo asked the same questions every time to hear the story. The only thing he'd never figured out was if it was out of her own interest to hear the glorification of her son or to remind Yuuki of the life debt he owed Jun.

But it didn't matter.

Yuuki had been lucky to survive when so many had died in the turf war. He might've exchanged sake cups with their new godfather, but Yuuki felt more loyalty to Jun than anyone else in the family.

"We need to get going," Jun said.

Yuuki wasn't finished, but he laid his chopsticks across his bowl.

Jun kissed his mother goodbye, and Yuuki thanked her again for the meal. They walked down the hallway and to the elevator in silence.

Jun tapped out a cigarette from his pack, and Yuuki lit it. Jun took a long drag, then blew out a stream of smoke.

"If you ever dare ask my mother questions like that again, I'm going to slit your throat and bathe in your blood."

"Of course. It was an accident," Yuuki apologized.

Jun smoked, and Yuuki said nothing the rest of the elevator ride. They walked out on the ground floor.

"You want to head to the club?" Jun asked. "We can find some girls desperate to get into the VIP section. It'll be fun. My treat."

"I want to make some headway on that app," Yuuki said.

"If that's what you want." Jun shrugged and gave Yuuki's shoulder a squeeze. "Try not to work too hard. It's your birthday after all."

They parted ways, and Yuuki grabbed the next train home. He rubbed his dry eyes. It was just a day like any other, even if on the inside his heart quivered.

He got off at his stop and walked the rest of the way to his apartment. It wasn't big, but the one-bedroom place was easy to clean, and his favorite coffee shop was across the street. He exchanged his contacts for glasses and opened to the next blank page in his journal.

He'd journaled every day since he was a kid. Within the pages, he could push through the most heinous days. He grabbed his favorite fountain pen and wrote.

He wrote about his lunch with his mother and her need to bring up grandchildren, again. Then the flowing lines of his words turned into sharp scratches when he reached meeting Kazuki. How when the back of his palm grazed Yuuki's chest, it had been the first time in ages he'd let another person get so close. Yuuki's skin had tingled like it had during their first study session. Kazuki had leaned in to give him a kiss, and that was how their relationship had turned deeper. On his birthday, Kazuki had made him a cake, and…

Fuck.

Yuuki didn't need to think about Kazuki like that. Sure, those memories left him buzzing, but Kazuki only ever did things to serve himself. He didn't care if his actions meant a bigger hassle for everyone around him as long as he felt good.

Yuuki didn't need to think about running his fingers through Kazuki's long hair or if his skin tasted of the same sweet salt.

The phone rang. His heart jumped to his throat. Jun? Kurosawa? The hospital? He reached for his phone.

The screen flashed. Mom.

Yuuki bit his lip.

He didn't want to pick up, but if he didn't, Mother would freak out and think something had happened.

"Hi, Mom. I'm downloading the app now," Yuuki said.

"Really?" She sounded shocked. "I'm so proud of you."

It wasn't like any of his relationships lasted very long. Once his boyfriends found out he was a yakuza, they always broke up with him. Even then, nothing would compare to the electric, anything-was-possible feeling he'd had with—

Yuuki wasn't getting any younger, and if it would make his mom happy, a sham marriage might be worth it.

Yuuki booted up his computer and went to the gay site he frequented. He clicked on the section for formal marriage requests and opened a new post.

Yuuki held his breath and hit Submit.

# chapter 6

*September 16*

Sporting his best jacket and tie, Kazuki headed to the only designer in Kyoto who'd replied to his collaboration email. Mrs. Noguchi's response had been lukewarm at best, but Kazuki would take what he could get.

Mrs. Noguchi was the owner/designer for an upscale women's clothing store. They both shared a love for quality fabrics, and if Kazuki could emphasize their shared interest, it could turn into the cornerstone of their collaboration.

He entered the shop.

A wave of lapis-blue garments popped against accents of ginger in her designs. The colors were thrown like a brazen act of rebellion, but with a single glance, Kazuki understood the hours of designing, fabric selection, and redrafting it took to look so effortless.

Even her store design and layout left him impressed. The crisp white on the walls emphasized the color of the store's selection. The windowed loft space above the sales floor led to Mrs. Noguchi's work studio.

He'd been inside her studio once before, a few weeks after his marriage. He and Hana had gone to every merchant in Kyoto to thank them for coming to their wedding and to present them with a piece of Hana's uchikake. The elaborately embroidered silk robe she'd worn over her kimono during the reception made for a perfect business card to showcase her family's craftsmanship. Hana had explained it as a family tradition since the late 1500s.

If Mrs. Noguchi thought Kazuki possessed even a pinch of Hana's creative genius, she'd jump at the opportunity for a collaboration.

"Welcome!" The store clerk gave Kazuki a cheerful greeting. Her black attire made the store's clothes around her sparkle like jewels. "What can I do for you?"

"Mrs. Noguchi's designs this season are stunning," Kazuki said. "Such bold choices of color. A bit different from mine, but I think the collaboration will push us both to new heights."

She gave a hesitant smile. "Was there something particular you were looking for? Maybe a gift for your girlfriend."

Kazuki laughed. "I'm actually here to see Mrs. Noguchi."

"Oh? She didn't tell me anyone was visiting."

"We've emailed each other about collaboration for the Kyoto fashion show."

"I see."

"Could you tell her I'm here? I'm Kazuki Okamoto. She knows me, I swear." He hated how desperate he sounded.

"I'll tell her." She hesitated. "But she's very busy this time of year."

The woman turned and headed toward the back in the opposite direction of Mrs. Noguchi's office.

"Wait," Kazuki called out. "She might remember me better as Kazuki Akamatsu."

"Akamatsu? Of course. I'll tell her right away. Follow me."

Kazuki followed the clerk upstairs, trying to swallow back the shame of dropping his ex-wife's name. Still, it got him an audience. The clerk motioned for him to wait on a chair outside Mrs. Noguchi's office while she entered.

A few moments of incomprehensible conversation filtered through the door, then a loud crack of laughter.

Kazuki flinched and brought a hand to his cheek. The burning prick of pain came, not from a slap, but from his teeth piercing his cheek. Whatever Mrs. Noguchi would say wouldn't be worse than the things he'd told himself.

The laughter cackled on.

The clerk opened the door and told Kazuki he could come inside. Mrs. Noguchi covered her face, hissing laughter escaping through her teeth.

"Shut the door behind you," she said.

He followed the direction and sat in the chair before the desk. She pulled her hand away from her face, and her rounded eyes bore into Kazuki's memories.

She hadn't just been another face attending their wedding. She had been the woman who'd pulled Kazuki aside and told him how lucky he was to marry Hana and be welcomed by her family.

"I can't believe you had the balls to come here after breaking Hana's heart," she said.

Kazuki clutched his hands. It didn't matter if he wore his best suit or his worst. His work couldn't escape his past.

"Our divorce was a mutual agreement." Kazuki's mantra gave him no strength. Not today. Not with her.

"As an Okamoto, you're nothing but the son of a tailor, but as an Akamatsu, you ascended into Kyoto's merchant royalty. A decade of apprenticeship with Hana, the foremost creative genius of her generation. And what did you do? You spat in the faces of one of the oldest and most prestigious families in Kyoto."

Kazuki pressed his lips together. He could design without Hana's influence. He'd done it for years. He'd built an established suit brand that needed to expand to a bigger store. He didn't need the Akamatsu name to create.

"I would like to collaborate with you." Kazuki kept his tone firm.

"The others might be too polite to say it, but someone needs to put you in your place."

"I have a few sketches I'd love to show you. Your bold style would make the perfect addition."

"Your schmoozing isn't going to work with me. I know what you did."

Kazuki's eyes narrowed. "What I did?"

"You knew Hana wanted children."

The tingling numbness began in his fingers, then spread all over his body. The room spun like a bobbin winder. His lips moved, but he couldn't push past the black hole of his nauseating agony to form words.

"Not only Hana, but every member of the Akamatsu counted on you." Mrs. Noguchi's voice stabbed. "And you went behind her back and got a vasectomy."

"What?" Kazuki blinked.

"Don't try to hide it. Everyone knows."

"That's not what happened."

"Whatever lies you want to tell to make yourself feel better won't work on me or anyone in the city." Mrs. Noguchi crossed her arms. "No one will collaborate with you. Not only because of what you did to Hana, but because you're in bed with the yakuza."

"Along with everyone who's worth mentioning in this city." Kazuki let out a sharp laugh and walked out of the office.

His grip tightened around the leather strap of his portfolio bag as he left the boutique.

Out of all the rumors about his relationship with Hana, the winner for what caused the divorce was him getting a secret vasectomy? How could something with only an ounce of truth become so twisted? If Mrs. Noguchi said it so matter-of-factly, no doubt the whole design community believed the lie.

The fashion show forbade designers outside the city from participating. Maybe a smaller indie designer would agree to the social risk and collaborate. Kazuki bit his lip. He didn't know any indie designers, and they would have totally different target markets.

Vague notions sprouted in his mind all the way back to his store but nothing worth harvesting. Kazuki came through the back staff entrance and found Fujio sitting at the sewing machine instead of Shizuri. He half-heartedly basted suit pieces together.

"One of them came," Fujio said. "So Shizuri's handling the measurements. She said I should do this."

"You'd go faster using a thimble." Kazuki motioned to the one sitting by the machine.

"That's what Shizuri said, but it's awkward, and I ended up going slower."

"In the long run, it'll be faster. Especially if you ever want to work as a sewer."

Fujio stopped and flashed a customer-service smile. "I haven't thought about sewing before."

"Would you want to?"

"I'm better at talking to people."

Too bad Fujio couldn't say two words to any yakuza.

"That's fine," Kazuki said through his teeth. "Here. Come with me."

They headed back to the office. Kazuki grabbed the

laptop off his desk, but the cord got caught on a stack of folders. A half dozen flipped over, their papers tumbling to the floor.

Kazuki sighed, stared at the stack, but turned back to the laptop.

"You can work here for now," Kazuki said.

Fujio stepped over the papers and sat in the chair. "What do you want me to do?"

"Post a job for sewers."

"I don't know how."

"Figure it out." It sounded harsh to Kazuki's ears, but he ignored it. "Find other listings and copy what they wrote. I need to organize these files. Again."

Kazuki scooped up the papers and dumped them onto the cutting table in the other room. He rolled his shoulders, not sure why they acted like he'd been hunched over a sewing machine all day.

He grabbed the first paper from the jumbled stack. Client measures, they all were, but they were completely out of order. Keeping them in a folder had seemed like a good idea at the time but not anymore. Coming up with a new system would take time, of which he had none.

He organized the papers in a steady rhythm but paused when he came to a page of measurements. Something familiar tugged at him like the thread being pulled on a whipstitch. He glanced at the name.

Yuuki…

Of course Kazuki had burned his ex's new measurements into his memory. Comparing the scrawny little bookworm Yuuki had been in high school to the measurements of the muscled Yuuki of today had become a new pastime.

Kazuki glanced at his sketchbook trapped underneath the paper maelstrom, then back to Yuuki's measurements.

Jun had paid for his suit to be rushed but not Yuuki's. His wouldn't be started for months.

Kazuki grabbed one of his favorite bolts of dark fabric—midnight coal with subtle gray threads. He should've been organizing the papers, sketching a new design, or even dispelling the rumors going around about him, but instead, he wanted nothing more than to make a suit for Yuuki.

# chapter 7



*September 17*

Yuuki knew Hokkaido would be cold, but he hadn't expected the blistering windy chill in September. He flipped up his jacket collar and waited outside the prison with the other visitors.

It would take a few months to broker the deal with the local mafia. Yuuki would be making the two-hour flight through the fall and into winter. He needed to buy a heavier coat, one not made by Kazuki.

A prison guard ushered the visitors inside and one by one wrote the names of who they were visiting.

"I'm here to see my Aunt Miko," Yuuki said.

"Last name."

As soon as Yuuki said it, the guard's crooked nose wrinkled, his eyes narrowed, and his required visitor smile turned into a scowl.

"Is she really your aunt, or are you one of those yakuza bastards?"

Yuuki's jaw clenched.

An ex-boyfriend had said the same thing when Yuuki had confessed his profession. *A yakuza bastard.* Yuuki couldn't be anything else to people outside the syndicate.

"Of course she's my aunt." Yuuki slapped on a false smile and handed over his family registry document.

The guard inspected the document like Yuuki had handed him a ransom note.

Yuuki rubbed his hands on his jeans. He'd ditched his usual yakuza uniform of suit and tie for normal street clothes to match the non-yakuza identity tailored for his family visit.

"Come with me." The guard huffed but didn't hand back the document.

They strolled farther away from the rest of the visitors, and every few feet, the guard glared back at him. They came to a small gray room with two metal chairs bolted to the floor.

"Sit."

Yuuki sat.

The guard shoved a tray in Yuuki's face. "Empty your pockets."

He handed over his wallet and phone, and the guard walked off with them. Alone in the windowless room, a shiver ran up Yuuki's spine.

No yakuza would freely walk into a prison, but he had, and he'd handed over his whole identity. Nothing would stop the guard from locking him up and throwing away the key.

The minutes passed.

Yuuki's foot bobbed. He wasn't meant to be doing something so important. After basic training, all his roles had always been managerial. Even the events that had led to Jun saving his life had been a case of the wrong place and wrong time.

The door opened, and Yuuki jumped.

A stupid smirk crossed the guard's face. "Follow me."

The guard escorted Yuuki to another tiny room. Two chairs and a table were bolted to the floor. A metal bar stuck to one end of the table, clearly for handcuffs. The only decoration in the room was a large sign on the wall that read *No touching.*

"Sit," the guard ordered.

A few silent and unnerving minutes later, Miko entered, escorted by her own guard. Yuuki had never seen his aunt without makeup. Miko's usual overdrawn lips were thin but still held a knowing grin. Her face was softer and rounder than the sculpted image of Yuuki's memory.

Still, these minor changes were nothing compared to the first time he'd seen Miko surrounded by the other yakuza officers. That day, Yuuki had stopped seeing her as the aunt who had secretly taken him out for ice cream every week in grade school and had started seeing her as someone who wouldn't flinch while doing whatever she needed to rise up the ranks.

Her guard cuffed her to the table and stood only a step away.

"Aunt Miko." Yuuki reached out to squeeze her hands.

"No touching!" the guard yelled.

Yuuki flinched and put his hands in his lap.

"They're serious about their rules here." Her authoritarian tone held a hint of mischief. "Anyway, happy belated birthday, nephew."

"Thanks. I know I should've visited sooner." Yuuki pressed his lips together. He wanted to get the business out of the way. "Hotels are expensive in Hokkaido, and I don't have any friends here that I can stay with."

"You'll have to start making some friends."

The mundane message was all Yuuki needed so the Kyoto mob could move forward and set up an alliance.

"Are they treating you well here?" Yuuki asked.

"They force me to sew clothes eight hours a day, but it could be worse. I could be doing more manual labor." Miko leaned back. "How's your mother? You can imagine they don't let me call her often."

"She's well. Cooked me a huge lunch for my birthday. Too bad you weren't able to come and help me eat it."

"You're her only child. She wants to spoil you."

"And ask about when I will give her a grandchild."

Miko laughed and waved her hand as much as she could cuffed to the table. "Give her a dog, and she'll be fine."

"Until next year."

"It'll be a few years before I can help rescue you from her prying into your personal life. You'll have to figure out how to stand up for yourself."

A weight pressed against his chest and his neck and his limbs. He'd always thought his aunt was on his side, but with the tightening in his throat, maybe he'd been mistaken.

"I'm actually thinking of dating," Yuuki said.

Miko raised a brow. "Oh?"

Yuuki had hoped telling his aunt would be good practice for when he'd tell his mom, but his stomach contorted into knots, and he couldn't get the words out.

He cleared his throat. "I joined one of those dating apps she keeps talking about."

"You know the kind of person you want to date?"

"I haven't really thought about it."

"You have to have an idea or else you'll end up only dating the wrong people."

Yuuki rubbed his face. "I just want her to be understanding."

"If that's what you want," Miko said, "make sure they're okay with your family."

He wanted his mother happy, and a sham marriage would

do it. Yuuki rolled his shoulders, sending a wave of pops echoing in his ears. Everything ached, whether from the flight, the metal chairs, or the pointed questions, Yuuki couldn't know.

"Time's up!" The guard glared at Yuuki. "You leave first."

Yuuki stood and shoved his hands into his pockets. The guard walked him down the hall, then stopped in front of the door where the other visitors were able to stay with their loved ones. Still, even if it was only ten minutes, it had been nice to see his aunt.

"When do I get my things back?" Yuuki asked.

The guard disappeared for a moment, then came back with the tray of Yuuki's personal items.

"Thanks." Yuuki reached out, but the guard turned the tray sideways. The items tumbled to the ground.

"Oops." The guard laughed.

He couldn't say anything, and the guards took full advantage of it just like the cops. If they'd been on the street, Yuuki would've decked him. Instead, he squatted and picked up his things.

Yuuki was escorted out of the prison, and from there, he walked the ten minutes to where Jun waited in the driver's seat instead of in his usual place in the back.

"Are you driving back to the airport?" Yuuki asked, sliding into his seat.

"Gotta practice sometime or else I'll forget," Jun said.

They stayed silent until the prison was far behind them.

"What did she say?" Jun asked.

"We can go ahead and start making an alliance with the local mob."

"We'll aim for a formal introduction in two weeks. Find a gift their godfather would enjoy."

"I'll see what else I can find out about the syndicate too. Did you help with the Tokyo alliance?"

"Ouch!" Jun laughed. "I'm not that old."

"Oh, I thought you went there to help with that hiccup."

"Sure, but I was more in the background in case shit hit the fan." Jun turned down a small street. "From what I hear, the Hokkaido family seems reasonable as long as Murata doesn't fuck it up."

Jun pulled into a parking spot.

"Wouldn't it be safer to eat at the airport?" Yuuki suggested.

Yuuki visiting his aunt in prison was one thing, but the street leader of another mafia walking around a city without prior contact was asking for disaster.

"We're stopping at an electronics store first. You were making that app, so you need to upgrade your setup."

"There's no need."

"You're helping me out, so let me return the favor. I don't know much about computers, but you always have my back."

"With a laptop, I could program on the plane."

"Good." But instead of getting out of the car, Jun squeezed the steering wheel. His Adam's apple bobbed as he swallowed. "My position is different from what I thought it would be."

Yuuki stayed silent. Jun kept Yuuki at a distance when it came to family. Father Murata hated Jun but didn't want to lose face in front of Yuuki because of his aunt. Jun had been an awesome ward leader or else Miko wouldn't have suggested him for a promotion.

"The higher you get, the more political it gets." Yuuki shrugged. "I admit, I like being a background player."

"Well, keep doing what you're doing. There's already been a significant increase in my club's profits thanks to you."

Yuuki's cheeks burned. "I haven't done much. So far just simple things like making sure the website had the right SEO."

"See? That's what I'm talking about. What the hell is SEO?"

"Well, it's when—"

Jun waved his hand. "I don't need to know since you do. Just keep it up. Now let's get you that laptop so you can make me even more money."

# chapter 8

Kazuki knew he shouldn't be in the workroom. He knew he shouldn't be hunched over a newly bought sewing machine. And he knew he shouldn't be crafting Yuuki's suit, but every time he opened his sketchpad or tried to tackle the pile of papers in his office, his fingers guided him back to the rich black fabric. Yuuki would wear something he created.

Shizuri came out of the office with a teacup in hand. She stood beside the sewing machine.

She didn't say anything, but she didn't need to.

"I know I need to rearrange the workroom so we can have two machines and the cutting table usable at the same time," Kazuki said.

She shrugged.

"And I know I should be working on the fashion show designs."

She sipped her tea.

"And I know it's stupid to be sewing, but I want to make this one." A tingling fluttered in Kazuki's stomach. "Yuuki was my boyfriend, and I—"

Shizuri spat out her tea. "Your boyfriend is a yakuza! No wonder we've been getting so many of them. Here I was thinking it was all because of that oolong tea junkie."

"No, no." The fluttering migrated from Kazuki's stomach to his heart. "Yuuki and I *were* a couple in high school. I hadn't seen him since graduation. We broke up on bad terms."

"I don't need to hear the sob story behind your apology suit. You want to sew. I don't care."

Shizuri's bluntness stung. Kazuki pressed his lips together. Whatever he said would result in another blow. It was stupid to feed the desire to be the one to make Yuuki's suit, but he couldn't press it down either.

Her eyebrows drew in. "But if you keep sewing hunched over like that, you're going to get a massive backache. A few years off a machine and you forget everything."

Shizuri set her teacup down and stood behind Kazuki.

"You have to sit straight and pull your shoulders back." She pushed Kazuki's shoulders into the proper sewing position. "There. Much better. Yuuki wouldn't want you getting a backache because of him. Though if the breakup was your fault, maybe Yuuki would want you getting a backache."

"At the time, I think he'd have been happy if I keeled over and died. He still might."

Shizuri hissed. "And I thought I had some bad breakups. It must've been something if he's still holding a grudge after all these years."

Kazuki waved his hand. "Better to overthink it and sew my way into a spiral."

"Or you don't spiral and put more paper in the fax machine."

"What?"

"It's out."

"Already? I put in paper the other day."

"Maybe it's time to look at them instead of letting them pile up."

"I'll get to it."

"After you finish the apology suit that doesn't need to get finished for months or when you get the designs for the fashion show finished?"

"I'm making progress on the designs."

Most of the designs simply turned into sketches of Yuuki, but it was more progress than he'd made in weeks.

The workshop door opened, and Fujio staggered inside. His eyes had widened to saucers, his skin as white as muslin. He fell into Shizuri's seat and covered his face with his hands.

"Th-there's another one." Fujio's voice shook through his hands. "It's… it's—"

Kazuki stood. "I'll take care of it."

Shizuri put a hand on his shoulder. "You're in the middle of a project. It's easier if I do it. Fujio, did you get their drink order?"

"Oolong tea."

A devouring silence ate through the space.

Only *one* person would ask for oolong tea.

Shizuri cleared her throat. "See? You're improving. You used to not be able to ask them anything."

She disappeared into the back, and Kazuki finished the seam. He glanced back toward Fujio, his face still buried in his hands.

"Do you want something to do so you can get your mind off Mr. Murata outside?"

Fujio said nothing. He did nothing.

Kazuki left Fujio to anguish alone and went to the

back office. He walked past Shizuri as she waited for the tea to steep.

"Why would Mr. Murata come without calling first?" Shizuri asked. "He always gets his secretary to call ahead."

"I don't know. Maybe it was a spur-of-the-moment thing."

"Or he hated his last suit, and we're all gonna die."

"Then you better make some damn good tea." Kazuki grinned and grabbed the stack of résumés off the fax machine.

"Good to know you think so highly of my tea." Shizuri laughed. "You really need to do something about Fujio."

"He's so great when it comes to the normal customers."

"Then do something about all the yakuza."

"Well, if your tea isn't up to snuff, we won't have to worry anymore."

"Very funny."

Shizuri threw out the steeped tea leaves and headed to the front. Kazuki checked underneath the fax cabinet for more paper, but there was none, and the angry red light on the machine kept flashing. Another thing to add to his to-do list.

Kazuki tapped the stack of résumés against the counter and headed back to the workroom. Fujio hunched over in his chair. He appeared so small. A far cry from the outgoing social butterfly he'd been when first hired. Dealing with the yakuza had snuffed out his flame.

Kazuki swallowed and placed the résumé stack in front of Fujio. "Look over these and pull the ones that stand out. It'll help distract you."

Fujio's hand quivered, but he pulled the stack into his lap. Kazuki went back to sewing, deciding to give Fujio space to gather himself.

A few minutes later, the paper crinkled in Fujio's hands.

"I can't do it," Fujio said.

"I know it's a huge stack," Kazuki said. "But each of these people took the time to send in their résumé. The least we could do is spend a few seconds looking it over."

"It's not the résumés. I can't do this."

"If you don't feel comfortable looking over résumés, we could use more paper."

"I quit." Fujio raised his head, eyes clear for once.

Kazuki blinked. "What?"

"I quit. I'm not coming back. I'll be much happier."

"I know those guys can look scary, but you can stay back here until you're comfortable. After the fashion show, we'll be back to normal customers."

Fujio dropped the résumés and walked out.

Kazuki stared at the empty chair, half expecting Fujio to come back, but why would he?

Kazuki hadn't done anything to detract any yakuza from coming into the shop. Sure, they'd been helpful in getting the bills paid, but with the huge surplus of orders, they'd be fine for months. Kazuki flipped the end of his hair against his finger. He'd allowed Fujio to suffer. All those days he'd been too scared to talk, his eyes glazed with a blank stare, Kazuki should've supported him instead of blaming it on everything else.

He couldn't get Fujio back, but Kazuki owed it to the next new hire to not put them through the same treatment.

Kazuki swallowed, but his throat still felt constricted.

All the merchants in Kyoto whispered the rumors about him and Hana to every customer who would consider coming to his store. To get to the root of the problem, he needed to confront his ex-wife.

Kazuki wrote a note for Shizuri to look over the résumés and left for the Akamatsus' kimono shop.

He'd thought the divorce had left him and Hana both happy with the results. The first year after their divorce, they'd even texted weekly. Sure, it had dwindled down to nothing over the next two, but Hana wouldn't start such a vicious rumor.

Would she?

No.

Hana was an amazing woman, a creative genius who would take him to some random festival around the city and turn around and conjure up two seasons' worth of designs. She'd made it easy to fall in love.

The Akamatsus' shop had stood in the same building in the historic city center for a hundred years. Their legacy ran deep.

A few luxury kimonos hung in the store's windows, one with gold-and-silver embroidery that only a geisha would wear. Inside, a few examples of kimono and yukata lined the wall, but most of the items were kept in the back.

For seventeen years, he'd worked at the shop in every position, a requirement from his father-in-law. As Kazuki stepped inside, a wave of nostalgia washed over him. It felt good, like coming home.

Yet instead of Kazuki being greeted with a hearty welcome, the man behind the counter's face grew red.

"You!" the man yelled.

Kazuki's eyes narrowed. The Akamatsu family business was one people spent years working for, but Kazuki had never seen the man before.

"I'm here to see Hana." Kazuki smiled. "I know she loves working in the back. Please tell her I only need a few minutes. She could keep working while we talk."

"You're not welcome here."

"This is a serious matter I need to discuss with her."

"She doesn't want to see you." The man puffed out his chest. "Not after what you did."

Kazuki left because what else could he do? Twice he'd failed, and the only thing left was for him to drown.

# chapter 9



Yuuki threw his paper coffee cup into the trash and switched his phone to his other ear. "Mom, I told you I joined the dating site."

"But you haven't gone on any dates yet."

Yuuki rubbed his temple and continued his stroll to the print shop. His mother's sudden *you-haven't-called-me-in-a-week-so-you-must-be-dead* phone calls had caught him by surprise. He had to answer; he just wasn't prepared for the interrogation.

"I'm not going to tell you about every little date."

"So you have gone on dates?"

"A few."

"That's wonderful."

Yuuki could hear her smile. His stomach twisted. He hadn't gone on any dates. He hadn't even gotten a response to his sham marriage post.

"I'll tell you when I find someone special," he said.

"Good. Find one that makes you happy. Oh! Peaches did the funniest thing the other day, or was it Lucky…"

He half listened while his mother continued their one-sided talk. She rattled off her activities from the week and the funny things the dogs were up to until he reached the yakuza-fronted print shop.

The anti-yakuza laws had gotten so strict that the Kyoto mob had set up the print shop so they could print everything from business cards to invitations. It acted as a completely legitimate business and allowed the mob to clean money.

He said goodbye to his mom and entered the small shop. Instead of a rousing welcome, he was greeted with silence. Yuuki wasn't in a rush, so he wandered around, flipping through a display of different card designs and inspecting a few filing cabinets for sale. His journey took him back to the front desk, where this time, he noticed a bell on the counter.

He rang it.

"Coming!" a familiar voice from the back said, but Yuuki couldn't place it until the man came into view.

"Pineapple!" Yuuki said. "It's been months."

They embraced, though Yuuki's arms couldn't fit around the stout Pineapple. His red cheeks only added to his cheerful demeanor. They'd been friends since Yuuki's new-recruit days.

"We would see each other more if you came out when I invited you," Pineapple said. "You used to come at least every few months."

"Well, you know."

"You used to go out all the time. Now you have wrinkles on your forehead."

"Everything with the war kept me busy." Yuuki shook his head. The excuse fit and meant he could avoid mentioning his mother's sickness. "When you said the family set you up with a cushy job, I didn't know it was at the print shop."

"Now the only thing I ever punch is the printer when it's not working." Pineapple let out one of his big belly laughs that always made Yuuki crack a smile.

"This place is close to my house. Maybe I'll try to visit again."

"If you do that, I'll have to start dressing fancy." Pineapple pressed down the wrinkles of his blue polo shirt. "I'm not used to important people coming here."

"I'm not that important."

"Who's your aunt again?"

Yuuki laughed. "I'm just the secretary. My to-do list consists of driving Jun around and picking up business cards." The new cards were needed to formally start the alliance talks with the Hokkaido mafia.

"Of course. I shouldn't keep you any longer. The cards are in the back. Let me get them for you."

Yuuki followed Pineapple because he really didn't mind the delay, especially for a friend he hadn't seen in months. Three large printers covered the back room. Pineapple grabbed two hand-sized boxes and slid them down the table to Yuuki.

"Are they to your liking?" Pineapple asked much too formally.

Yuuki pulled out one of Jun's thick black linen cards with gold-foil text. Yuuki's were white with the simple word *secretary* under his name.

"They look too fancy, knowing you made them," he said.

"I only put the paper in the machine. Now how can I guilt you into going out with the guys this weekend?"

"I might be busy." Yuuki stuffed the cards back into their boxes. "I started dating again."

"Dating?" Pineapple rubbed his mustache. "I always thought you were asexual."

"Asexual? What made you think that?"

"Well, you never went home with anyone."

The room tilted, the heat of the printers hitting Yuuki like a fireball. He leaned against the counter to steady himself. Pineapple always had Yuuki's back, but being called asexual had hit too close to home.

Since joining the mob, Yuuki had carefully crafted each move. Not taking any men home, not staring at any guy a little too long, and when he had boyfriends, they'd always gone to places not frequented by family members.

"I'm not going to go home with some random girl I met at a club. She could turn out to be a psycho." Yuuki scoffed, hoping it sounded believable. "But my dating post hasn't gotten any replies, so maybe I can go out with you guys. Where are you thinking of heading? The usual place?"

Pineapple raised a brow. "Did you go back in time? Who makes a post asking for dates?"

"It's a website where people make posts. It doesn't have all those distracting ads or pictures, just information. My mom's back on her grandchildren kick, so I'm trying to find a woman to marry, not some casual hookup."

"Okay, that makes sense. You get to know her before seeing a photo. But you're a good guy. Why has no one messaged you? Did you even try in your post?"

Yuuki crossed his arms. "I tried."

"Let me see."

"You don't need to see my dating profile."

"I want to see this empty mailbox you say you have."

Yuuki pulled out his phone and showed his empty email account. "See? No one replied."

"You really wanted a date, huh? You didn't even check your spam folder." Pineapple snatched the phone out of Yuuki's hand, then whistled. "Hello, nurse."

"What are talking about?"

"She says she works at a hospital. You guys can go play doctor when you meet her."

"Just because she messaged me doesn't mean she wants to go on a date."

"She says she wants to speak business with you when you're available." Pineapple wiggled his eyebrows. "She moves fast. I like it."

"Let me see that." Yuuki snatched his phone back.

"Go ahead and message her. Tell her she has pretty eyes. Ladies like that. Maybe send her a picture."

"She didn't send me a photo. Why would I say she has pretty eyes when I don't even know what she looks like?"

"Say it on the date. When is the date? She messaged you last week. You better reply quickly or else she'll think you're a jerk."

"I'll do it later."

"I believe that as much as the police believe this is a legitimate business."

"Fine," Yuuki deadpanned and replied with a quick message.

Pineapple beamed. "I want to know how the date goes."

"Sure, sure. I need to get going."

"Important family work is never done."

"More like I need to get fitted for a fancy suit to impress the boss."

"Fancy new position comes with a fancy new suit."

"Believe me, if it weren't a gift, I wouldn't be going to any damn fitting."

Yuuki grabbed the business card boxes and said goodbye. He headed to the other side of town by train. He distracted himself from his thoughts about Kazuki by arranging the next flights to Hokkaido and gathering information about the local godfather. Yet as he got off the train and headed to

Kazuki's store, Yuuki's stomach churned, his thoughts trapped between frustration over what Kazuki had done and the excitement of having Kazuki's hands on his body.

Yuuki swallowed and entered the store. Kazuki came out from the back, tying his long hair back with an elastic band. The sleeve of his oxford shirt was rolled up. Yuuki must've been staring because Kazuki mumbled an apology and rolled down his sleeve.

"Thanks for coming in for the first fitting." Kazuki's voice hung with exhaustion. "Is there something you'd like to drink?"

Yuuki waved his hand. "I'm fine."

"Could you wait for me in the fitting area while I grab your suit?" Kazuki spoke so informally he could've stepped out of Yuuki's memory.

Yuuki found his way to the seating arrangement and reminded himself of Kazuki's past transgression and not how hot his arms looked. Kazuki returned, holding a clothing bag and with his shirtsleeves securely buttoned.

"Sorry I didn't have the suit already prepared for you." Kazuki unzipped the bag. "I'm warning you ahead of time. The suit is going to look like a mess right now. We need to keep areas temporarily sewn to make for easier adjusting. After this fitting, it will look more like a real suit."

"I see."

Yuuki slid his coat off and tossed it over the chair as Kazuki messed around with getting the full three-piece suit out. Yuuki unbuckled his pants next and slid them off.

Kazuki turned back. His eyes widened, and a small flush covered his face and neck. A slow smile crossed Yuuki's face.

"We have a changing room over there." Kazuki gestured to the curtained room behind him.

"You've seen me in less."

Kazuki gave a little laugh. "I wasn't expecting you to undress in front me of. I thought you hated me."

"I can hate you and still be attracted to you."

Kazuki opened his mouth but said nothing, his eyes cast down. Maybe Yuuki could've said it a little nicer or not at all. He couldn't deny the attraction between them, and he couldn't help but tease Kazuki. Especially since in high school, it had been Kazuki who'd done the teasing.

Yuuki buttoned the last button of his vest and slid on the coat. "I'm ready for you to go ahead and grope me"

Kazuki paused, staring at Yuuki, then took a step closer. His golden eyes lingered over Yuuki's body before snapping up to meet Yuuki's.

Kazuki pressed his lips together. "I'm not trying to touch you. Your sleeves are a little off." Kazuki carefully turned a sleeve, broke a few stitches, then laid the fabric flat. "How much of your shirt do you like showing?"

Yuuki closed his eyes, kicking himself for sounding so… desperate. "Most people don't have opinions about how much shirt they show."

"You'll be surprised. Do you like this or this more?" Kazuki moved the fabric to show more or less of the sleeve.

"Longer is fine."

Kazuki pinned down the fabric, his fingers not once grazing Yuuki's skin. Each moment, Yuuki wished he would a little more.

"Studying late?" Yuuki smiled.

"What?"

"Those dark circles underneath your eyes remind me of when we'd stay up late studying. When we were actually studying."

"Someone quit, so it's double the work. I was up sewing. Nothing as fun as our study sessions."

"Doing what was easy for yourself instead of doing what was right again."

"It doesn't matter, not anymore at least. I think the waist can be taken in a bit more, like this." Kazuki stuck in a few more pins. Again carefully avoiding any lingering touch. "Now you can see how trim you are."

"That does look nice." Yuuki's stomach grumbled, and he laughed. "Do you know a good restaurant around here?"

"There's a good eel place."

"Expensive taste."

"We deal with expensive suits."

Yuuki licked his bottom lip. "You still have the same confidence as before."

"It's no wonder I was elected class president."

"More like you handed candy to everyone moments before it was time to vote."

"The others running could've handed out candy."

"I didn't have to."

"Because no one else wanted to be secretary."

"There was a line where they could've written someone else. Clearly, my platform of organized notes for easy reference for all won them over."

They both laughed.

Kazuki made everything feel so easy. Talking, joking, even the trips down memory lane didn't contain the same rocky bumps. Yuuki couldn't deny the tingling inside him. Maybe seventeen years was too long to carry a grudge. He was only hurting himself.

"I think once you wear the suit a few times, you'll see the benefit of having something made for you," Kazuki said. "It'll be small things at first. You'll realize you don't have that tight feeling in the shoulders, or you'll notice how people treat you with more respect. I promise after wearing one of mine, you'll want me to dress you for every occasion."

Yuuki stripped out of the clothes, loving the way Kazuki looked away but was clearly side-eyeing him. He handed the clothes one by one to Kazuki, but when they got to the final pair of pants, their fingers touched. A second was fine, but they both lingered a little longer than they should have.

Kazuki pulled away, turning to hang up the pants. "You still watch baseball?"

"The Tigers are really killing it this season." Yuuki tucked his shirt into his pants.

"Maybe we can meet up and watch a game together."

Yuuki bit his tongue before saying anything. It had been years since he had a friend he was out to. Rekindling a connection with Kazuki would be like switching from a hard disk to a solid-state drive, faster and without having to calculate every action to appear straight. It sounded easier than rejoining Pineapple and their bar outings. Even if a friendship with Kazuki didn't last, at least it would replace the bitter memories from high school.

"Why not start today?" Yuuki said. "We can go to the eel—"

The shop door opened, and Yuuki stepped away from Kazuki in case a family member walked in, but it wasn't a yakuza. A woman in a bright red and orange kimono entered. Yuuki would never forget her bigger-than-the-moon eyes and bow lips.

"Hana?" Kazuki said under his breath.

"I don't care if the suit isn't perfect," Yuuki hissed. "Send it to my house. I'm not coming back."

# chapter 10

When Kazuki and Yuuki had touched, Kazuki's whole body had buzzed with a flourish of old memories colliding with the electric antici- pation of new ones. Yuuki must've felt the same or else he wouldn't have gotten that little smirk on his face. Kazuki could've kissed him, but then Hana had entered the shop.

"Yuuki, wait!" Kazuki called, but the door shut with Yuuki on the other side.

Kazuki sighed.

His ex-wife stood by the counter. Somehow, she'd packed her vast creative genius into a body that only came up to Kazuki's chest. Her black hair was tied up with a floral comb matching the fall colors of her kimono. Her obi sat a little higher than usual to accommodate her pregnant belly.

"I can come back later if now's not a good time," Hana said.

"It's fine." Kazuki rubbed his neck. "My dating life has been nonexistent. I don't know why I thought trying to get back with Yuuki would go any differently."

"The guy who wrote all those notes?"

"Same Yuuki, more muscles."

A year into their marriage, Hana had come out of their bedroom holding the box where Kazuki had kept the daily notes Yuuki would stuff into his shoe locker or trade with him after lunch. No matter how much Kazuki had tried, he couldn't let them go. She had been reading them like a novel, and the pained look on her face had pushed Kazuki to confess his sexuality for the first time.

"Maybe it's fate you two are reconnecting," she suggested.

"More like a curse."

"They can feel similar." Hana shifted her weight between her feet and rested her hand across her stomach.

"Let me get you a chair. I shouldn't make a pregnant woman stand," Kazuki apologized.

"Don't start with that. I hear enough of it back at the shop."

"They all must be excited to have another Akamatsu coming into the world."

"Excited, yes. Overbearing, also yes. You carry a baby and suddenly everyone thinks you can't do anything yourself anymore. I can't even make a cup of tea without someone stopping to help."

Kazuki laughed. "That must be challenging, especially for you."

"Akio will faint when he finds out I walked here all by myself."

"Akio? Is he the new front clerk?"

"Yes, and my husband."

Kazuki's eyes widened. He should've been happy to know Hana had moved on. Logically, he was happy, thrilled even. Emotionally, the juxtaposition against his utter failure when it came to relationships over the past three years left a bitter taste lingering in his throat.

"Found one that doesn't shoot blanks," he blurted. "Sorry, I…"

"He knew how important children were to my family, so he got everything checked out before proposing."

"Ah," Kazuki said since suggesting his ex-father-in-law had no doubt forced the groom would be inappropriate. "How long have you been married?"

"Ten months."

"He works fast too." Kazuki slapped his hand over his mouth. "Sorry, this is just odd. Seeing you like this and knowing everything."

"I could see how this could be hard *for you*." Hana's words instantly put Kazuki's feelings into perspective.

Of course Hana wouldn't care how awkward it was for him. She'd gotten everything she wanted in the end. Kazuki had walked away with enough alimony to open his shop and a reputation as the worst man in Kyoto.

Kazuki twisted the end of his hair. "Do you know anything about that rumor going around about me?"

"Actually—"

The door opened, and Hana silenced the rest of her sentence between her pink lips.

Business came first. It had always had. Her family lineage went deep, mandating her and Kazuki's smiling presence at many events throughout the city.

Kazuki greeted his three o'clock fitting, another yakuza, lower ranking he guessed from the slim order of only a jacket. He got the client's drink order and ushered Hana to the back workshop. He asked Shizuri to take over dealing with the client.

Hana stepped into the office and laughed. "Kazuki, really?"

"What?" He grabbed the stack of papers resting on the chair and moved them to his desk.

"This is a disorganized mess even for you."

"I haven't had time to clean."

Hana rubbed her temple. "It's spring cleaning all over again."

"You'd always put everything into so many boxes. It took forever to find something."

"If you'd actually read the labels, you wouldn't have had to open up ten." Hana picked at the pile of button-down shirts covering the liquor in the kitchenette, exposing the bar. "You're drinking on the job?"

"It's for the customers." Kazuki grabbed the shirts and put them someplace less noticeable, which didn't exist, so he put them someplace behind Hana so she wouldn't notice.

"You make shirts too?"

"No. We're hiring a new sewer. Figured the easiest way was to give them a stipend and have them create a shirt from my measurements."

"I see. You had them do shirts since it's the easiest to see who is the most skilled."

"Exactly." Kazuki brushed off his office chair with his hand and presented the seat to Hana.

"Thanks." Hana sat, looking around the room as if trying to find the most organized place to rest her gaze. Then she sighed and looked at her sleeve. "We've had an uptick in yakuza clients as well."

"Really?"

"Their new godfather likes to wear yukata. So now we have lots coming in to buy one. Good thing most don't want anything custom, so they're in and out in no time."

"If only it could be so easy here."

"It'll eventually stop coming, and you'll be back to normal

overpaid businessmen. Anyway, I came by because I wanted to extend an apology for my husband's behavior when you came into my shop."

"Thanks." Kazuki crossed his arms. "Do you know anything about the rumor going around about me?"

"I never told anyone you were bisexual if that's what you heard."

"People are saying I broke your heart by getting a vasectomy."

Hana laughed. "You didn't need a vasectomy."

"But do you know who could've started it?"

"How on earth would I know—" Her eyes widened. "Father."

"You really think he'd say that?"

"It sounds like him, doesn't it?"

Knowing his ex-father-in-law, the man probably thought the rumor would protect Kazuki's manhood while allowing his daughter to save face.

"Now every business owner in Kyoto hates my guts," Kazuki said.

"They'll stop once people realize I'm not mad at you. That's why they hid your application for the Kyoto fashion show the past two years."

"They what?"

"I've been on the board accepting the applications. This year, I realized they'd all been secretly voting no on your application without doing the formal review so I wouldn't have to feel uncomfortable. It was sweet if you think about it. But I told them I was excited to see your designs. Speaking of which"—she tapped her fingers on the desk—"you came up with a few nice yukata designs. Since I'm here, I'd love to see what you're working on."

"But it's not fixed. I've been trying to find a collaborator for weeks, and I get nothing back. Mrs. Noguchi yelled at me about getting a vasectomy so we could never have kids."

"Then collaborate with me. Once people see our names together at the fashion show, no one will think I'm mad at you anymore, and we can come up with designs no yakuza would want. It's perfect."

Kazuki blinked, a weight lifting off him. "You really mean it?"

"I wouldn't be saying it if I didn't. Hopefully, the collaboration doesn't change your designs too much."

"I've been too swamped with clients to even organize the office let alone design."

"Then we'll have a fun three months creating. After the baby's out, you're on your own."

"That's perfect." Kazuki grabbed the sketchbook and turned to the next blank page. "Let's get started now."

# chapter 11

*October 2*

Yuuki tightened his grip on the steering wheel and drove out of sight of the Kyoto yakuza headquarters, his gaze on the streets, Jun's jiggling foot, and the tiny pieces of porcelain trapped in his hair.

"Fuck!" Jun punched the glove compartment.

Kazuki had done an impeccable job with Jun's suit. The tailored lines and snug fit somehow aged Jun's baby face from a high school student's to a college grad's. It had impressed Yuuki, but Father Murata?

Never.

A moth trapped in a jar would have had a better chance of surviving the meeting with Father Murata than Jun. He swallowed, unable to find the right words to console his boss. Yuuki had no idea how to please their new godfather. No one did.

"He threw a fit because he saw graffiti on a building and thought it was from the Korean mafia." Jun massaged his reddening knuckles. "What kind of godfather would bring up something so mundane and blame me for not keeping the ward leaders on a tight enough leash to stop it?"

"You'll only have to put up with him for five years, then Miko will be released," Yuuki said.

"I swear, one day I'm going to punch him square in the jaw."

"Murata boxes in the mornings."

Jun laughed, and the stiff mood in the car lightened.

"Where do you want me to go?" Yuuki asked.

"Historic district. We're going to pick up some yukata. If the suit doesn't work, maybe attending one of the festivals will."

Yuuki glanced at the clock. "Do you think it'll take long?"

"Why, you got a hot date?"

"I can rearrange it if necessary."

Jun's eyes widened for a moment, but then a toothy grin crossed his face. "I can select a yukata for you. Park the car outside the historic district then go on your date. Your mom wants grandchildren."

"A first date is a long way from grandkids."

"If you get lucky, it might not be. You want to make your mom happy, right?"

"Of course." Yuuki swallowed, staring into the backseat window of the car in front of him. A little kid's head bounced into view with the occasional action figure flying in the air. "I never saw myself as the married with children type."

"You're a man. It's not as much work for you. How many memories do you have of your father that don't involve him reading the newspaper or yelling at the TV."

"You can avoid a screaming baby. I should find a woman who already has a child."

Jun sucked air through his teeth. "Your mother doesn't want that. She wants to see what parts of you made it into the child. She can't do that with some stepchild."

"Oh."

Yuuki's hands squeezed the wheel. If what Jun said was true, then Yuuki's plans for a fake marriage were hopeless. His stomach twisted like the unkempt wires in the back of a computer. He wanted to grab a zip tie and hook all the elements of his life together to make his mother happy, but how permanent of a solution did he need? How much longer would his last?

Once they arrived outside the historic district, Yuuki parked, and Jun wished him good luck on his date.

Yuuki had enough time to return home and change into something more casual. The off hour on a Thursday afternoon made her easy to spot since she was the only customer there. Sara wore an emerald shirt. Her brown hair was tied back in a tight ponytail. It was a reasonable length, unlike Kazuki's.

Yuuki bit his tongue. He shouldn't be thinking about Kazuki. Not now.

"Sara?" Yuuki asked.

"Yup. You must be Yuuki."

"Sorry I'm late, I was…" Yuuki trailed off. He'd said he was unemployed, so he couldn't say he had a surprise meeting with the local yakuza godfather that had messed up his schedule.

"You're fine. I got here early." The confident lilt in her voice made Yuuki feel like his shoes were too big.

He stood by the empty chair in front of her. She took

another sip of her drink. Her red lipstick left a mark on the rim.

"I'll get a drink," Yuuki said. "Do you want anything?"

She held up her paper cup. "I'm good. It's not a real date, so don't feel obligated to get me anything."

"Right, sorry."

Yuuki grabbed himself a coffee and a piece of chocolate mousse cake, figuring it would give him time to think without the silence turning awkward. The upbeat chorus of a pop song played on the café's stereo, but the lighthearted mood didn't ease Yuuki's apprehension.

Yuuki sat at the table. "So you're a nurse?"

"No. I'm a brain surgeon."

"Oh, sorry. I shouldn't have assumed." Yuuki took a bite of his cake.

"Happens all the time." She waved her hand. "My medical test scores were so good they wouldn't dare lower them."

"Why would they lower test scores?"

"It's not proven, but everyone knows it happens. They lower women's test scores. They're too concerned we'll get pregnant and leave the profession."

"My mother keeps talking about grandchildren. I can imagine it would double if I were a woman."

"My parents talk about grandchildren, too, but don't worry. I have the solution once we're married."

Yuuki choked on his cake. He coughed, grabbing his coffee.

"Your post did say you were looking for a woman to have an in-name-only marriage. It's business. Why sugarcoat it?" Her words came fast and clinically like the time the doctor had insisted on same-day surgery after his mom's seizure.

"You're right." Yuuki's tongue burned. "This is business. My mother had it rough last year. I know this marriage will make her happy."

"We'll say the other can't have children, and it'll solve the grandchildren problem."

Would simply being married be enough to make his mother happy?

"You live with her?" Sara asked.

"I have my own place."

"But you said you were unemployed?"

"It's not so much unemployment. I program, but it's here and there."

"Freelance. I see." She crossed her arms. "That does change things."

"How so?"

"I wanted a kind of house husband. I have an extra room where you can sleep and live rent-free if you agree to clean and cook. You can imagine coming home after thirteen hours of surgery I don't want to do any of that. You seem nice from all the emails back and forth. Would you be up for that?"

Yuuki couldn't eat enough cake to fill the silence, but he eventually spoke. "I do like living by myself."

"Well, here's my final proposal. You can keep your place or even move into mine. I don't care what you do. Just know my family likes to do surprise visits, so if I call, you're going to have to stay over and play pretend. We'll tell them you sleep in the other room because of my crazy hospital hours. I can do the same for you."

"Isn't this a little fast?"

"Why wait? You checked the last one of my boxes. How do I look with yours?"

"My boxes?"

"You do have a list of what you want out of this marriage, correct?"

Yuuki smashed the last crumb of cake with his fork. "You're actually the first person I talked to about this."

Sara took the final sip of her coffee. Yuuki stared at the last bite of his cake. Jun was right. Yuuki owed his mother everything, so it was only right for him to make her happy. Everything Sara asked for amounted to some paperwork and a few days a year playing pretend. It wasn't bad, but then why did Yuuki hesitate so much?

"Give me some time to think about it," Yuuki said.

# chapter 12



*October 16*

By the time Kazuki arrived at the Kamigamo shrine, the festival was already in full swing. The horseback riding archers had already begun their competition. They each took turns shooting at progressively smaller targets. It was a small festival compared to the others the city offered, and being in the middle of the week didn't help attendance. Even in the back, Kazuki had a decent view.

Hana had suggested the festival outing to gain inspiration. The bright blues, pinks, and golds of the costumed noble reenactors complimented her fabrics, while the powerful stances and thundering horses captured the masculine lines of Kazuki's suits. He took out his sketchbook along with small swatches of fabric Hana had offered up for her part of the collaboration. He scratched out a few rough lines, the standard male-framed figure.

The minutes passed, his attention bouncing between rider, fabric, and paper. Once all the archers finished the set, Kazuki glanced down at the sketchbook.

Yuuki.

"Damn it," Kazuki said under his breath.

He thought he would get over the every-sketch-is-like-Yuuki phase once Hana brought the samples. He rubbed his face. He had years of sketches without Yuuki popping into his designs, but the man shows up twice, and suddenly, he's permanently pinned to Kazuki's creative subconscious. Yuuki wanted nothing to do with him, and the sooner Kazuki removed the pin, the better for his aching heart.

He flipped to the next blank page and caught sight of a small gap in the crowd up front. His mind couldn't wander with the horses an arm's length away.

Kazuki weaved his way through and claimed his spot next to a small group dressed in traditional indigo yukata. Perhaps no one got close because they appeared to be part of the show.

The first archer for the next round galloped by. The air rushed over him. His heart thumping louder than horse hooves.

"You need to take a step back," a man growled.

Kazuki turned back toward the man. No one but a yakuza would wear a suit darker than pitch to such a lively event. The local yakuza crest was pinned to his lapel.

"I'm sorry. I didn't mean any offense," the words dripped from Kazuki's mouth. "I'll go."

"It's fine." Kazuki recognized the voice, even if he didn't want to believe it.

He gulped as his gaze became impaled by the haunting nightmare of Mr. Murata's crow-dark eyes.

"Mr. Okamoto, it's always a pleasure. Have you come to watch the archery too?" Mr. Murata's formal tone did not hide the knife-sharp lilt in his voice.

"Ah, yes." Kazuki cleared his throat, hoping to hide his panic. "I apologize for interrupting. I was sketching some new ideas using the festival as inspiration. I didn't mean to disturb you. I'll be on my way."

"Nonsense, you can get a better view here with us."

Us?

Kazuki's eyes widened, finally noticing the other members of the group. Mr. Murata's secretary stood beside him followed by Jun, then Yuuki. The narrowness of his eyes screamed for Kazuki to leave.

"I wouldn't want to impose," Kazuki said.

"I insist." Mr. Murata's smile appeared more death threat than reassuring. "I would feel personally offended if you did not join us. There's a good spot." He motioned to the empty space beside Yuuki.

"It would be a great pleasure to join you." Kazuki masked his nervous laugh underneath formal platitudes.

He took his place beside Yuuki. His muscles twisted like thread wrapped around a bobbin. He swallowed, and his heart trembled.

Yuuki in a suit.

Yuuki in a yukata.

Kazuki couldn't tell which was more alluring.

He clutched his sketchbook, catching Yuuki's features from the corner of his eye. The male figure in the sketch grew, with wider shoulders, a trimmer waist, and a filled-out face. A man, not a lanky high schooler. His hair was longer and swept back. The graphite of the pencil was unable to capture the right tempting brown of Yuuki's eyes.

"Really?" Yuuki hissed.

Kazuki hid the drawing's face underneath the swatch of fabric and put down a few arbitrary lines to make up the suit. He continued the charade until Yuuki's attention returned to the horses.

Kazuki ran his fingers through his hair to block the

others from view. Kazuki's skin burned, but he couldn't tell if it was simply from Mr. Murata's presence or because Yuuki stood so close. Every time Kazuki tried to move away, Mr. Murata would glare at him, and Kazuki stepped back in line.

After three more rounds of target shooting, Kazuki was able to excuse himself to hide in the restroom.

Kazuki sloshed water onto his handkerchief then lifted his hair to press the cloth against his neck. He wouldn't be surprised if steam came off how fried his nerves felt. He rolled his shoulders and rounds of pops squeezed out with each movement.

He needed to concentrate. He'd rearranged the day's clients so he could sketch at the tournament, but at this rate, he'd fill a sketchbook without creating a single design.

Kazuki cupped his hands under the sink and splashed the cool water on his face.

The door squeaked open.

Then the distinct *click* of the lock echoed through the room.

Kazuki's throat tightened. Yuuki leaned against the only exit, arms crossed, his brilliant eyes a smear of cold isolation.

Kazuki gulped.

All the other times he'd set eyes on Yuuki, he could see the high-school boy he'd loved underneath the muscle and swagger, but not anymore. For the first time, Yuuki actually looked like a yakuza, a dark monster of the underworld.

Kazuki took a step back. "I tried to leave. I swear."

"What part of I don't want to fucking see you again do you not understand?" Yuuki growled.

"Honestly, I was only here to sketch."

"Sketch designs of me."

"They were designs, I swear." The desolation in Kazuki's

voice scared him. The inferno blazing in Yuuki's eyes scared him more. "I have fabric samples—"

"Do you know how hard it is for me to see your stupid face?" Yuuki punched through the hollow wooden door to the only bathroom stall.

Kazuki flinched.

Yuuki pulled back a bloody fist. "Or how hard it would be for me if someone found out I'm gay?"

No matter how much Yuuki tried to disguise his tone, Kazuki knew him well enough to hear the terror underneath.

"Yuuki…"

"Don't speak!" Yuuki said between clenched teeth. "If I ever see your face again, you'd better run."

Kazuki closed his eyes, but inside, he wasn't trembling with fear. He wanted to take Yuuki in his arms and say he'd be fine, how he knew putting on an act for so long would drive anyone mad, but more than anything, he wanted to beg Yuuki to call his name.

# chapter 13

*October 24*

"Wait here," the prison guard ordered.

Yuuki rubbed his hands together and tried to ignore the chill from the prison's metal chair. Visiting his aunt brought a smile to his face, but he'd never get used to the taunting expressions worn by the guards. Once Father Murata drank sake with the Hokkaido don, Yuuki wouldn't have to step foot in the prison again.

A guard walked Miko into the room and pushed her into the chair. Yuuki winced. Dark circles hung under her eyes, and her jumpsuit hung a little more loosely than Yuuki remembered.

"I'd bring you some better to food, but they won't let me give you anything," Yuuki said.

Miko smiled. "I never knew food could taste gray, but enough about me. How was your mom's follow-up appointment?"

"It's not until next month."

"Let's hope it's better this time. I worry about her

sometimes. Probably because it's better than worrying about all this."

"I have more good news." Yuuki's gaze drifted to the clock on the opposite wall. "I'm getting married."

"You met a girl in Hokkaido?" she asked. "Too bad I won't be able to attend the ceremony."

Yuuki swallowed. The banal way Miko spoke meant she thought he was talking about the alliance. Yuuki could've been talking about the weather instead of a major life decision. Her expression was unfazed, her arm holding up her head in such a way to avoid the bruise.

"No, not in Hokkaido," Yuuki corrected. "A woman back home."

"But it was only last month you said you were only thinking about dating."

"When you find someone, and you know it's right, why not jump in?" Yuuki's tone sounded too forced to be believable.

Her eyes narrowed. She tapped her fingers against the table. If she could smoke, she'd be a crematorium pipe.

"Did your mom arrange it?" Miko asked.

"I don't want to be with a friend of a cousin from one of her mah-jongg friends."

"Did she bump into you someplace you always go? Are you sure of her intentions?"

"We met online. She messaged me on a dating app."

"Are you sure she's not Korean?"

Yuuki pressed his lips together, taking a moment to work through Miko's true meaning. She didn't care about the ethnicity of the girl but still warned him she could be a Korean spy.

"Sara's not Korean. She's a brain surgeon." His tongue burned saying her name out loud.

"She hasn't met your family, has she?"

Another layered question that twisted Yuuki's stomach like a Möbius strip. Miko's calculated question echoed the flaw in all Yuuki's relationships. Anytime he'd confessed his profession, it spelled the end.

No one wanted to date a yakuza.

"She hasn't met anyone yet," Yuuki said. "We're still talking about housing arrangements. She has her own condo, bigger than my place. We don't want a fancy wedding, so it'll be quick. Maybe I'll be married the next time I see you."

"She has to meet your family first. She should've met them before you proposed."

"She actually proposed."

"That's even worse."

Yuuki opened his mouth to protest, then shut it. He concealed parts of himself from his aunt, but he never lied to her, and she'd always been brutally honest with him. Especially given the limitations his family brought to his future.

"I like Sara," Yuuki said. "Marriages have been built on less."

Miko should've been happy. Instead, her eyebrows knitted together, and her nails tapped against the table like a war drum.

"Stop being delusional," she snapped. "You should have told Sara before you agreed."

Maybe he hadn't thought the sham marriage through. Sara would ruin her career by marrying a yakuza. Yuuki couldn't keep it a secret until after they were married. Maybe he needed to find a woman with a lower-status job.

Even if a woman didn't care Yuuki was a yakuza, she wouldn't want to have children with him. But marriage would be the first step. Yuuki could say they were trying to start a family, and if his mother took a turn for the worst, at least she could die with hope.

"I never married, and I'm not having kids." Miko's caustic tone burned. "The people around me became my family."

"Mother deserves some happiness, especially after everything she went through last year. I want to make her happy."

"Worry about your own happiness."

"I want to get married."

She sighed. "I thought someone as smart as you wouldn't be so dumb."

Yuuki frowned, and Miko reached out to squeeze Yuuki's hand.

"No touching!" the guard yelled and yanked Miko from her chair. Her cuffed wrist popped.

Yuuki winced.

"Don't do something you'll regret for the rest of your life."

—

Yuuki fished his keys out of his pocket and climbed the remaining flight of stairs to his apartment. The frosty twilight darkness of the ending day marked each exhale of breath.

A large box stood propped up against his door. Yuuki ignored the package and let it fall inside the apartment, then kicked it over the threshold.

He plopped onto his bed and dialed Sara's number.

The phone rang, but Sara's voicemail message clicked on, telling Yuuki if he was in a medical emergency to hang up and dial 1-1-0.

"Hi, Sara. It's Yuuki." He licked his lips. His aunt's words buzzed in his ears. "Let's meet again. Text me when you're next free."

He hung up and dragged the package to his bed. He grabbed the knife off his desk and sliced open the box. Inside was another box, but this one was crisp white with a red bow tied around it.

His suit.

Yuuki rubbed his temple, debating about shoving it into the corner and forgetting about it, but Jun would ask why he wasn't wearing it.

"Might as well get it out of the way," he said, giving himself the little pep talk he needed to move forward.

He pushed back the tissue paper, then narrowed his eyes. Nestled on top of the midnight fabric was a collection of paper. Notes. A wave of countless memories washed over him.

In high school, he and Kazuki were in different classes. They'd ritualistically exchange notes during their shared lunch and stuff them into each other's shoe locker. Yuuki had trashed his notes from Kazuki ages ago, but Kazuki had kept his… until now.

Why would Kazuki have kept them all this time?

Yuuki pressed a hand to his chest. His heart thumping rapidly against his rib cage made his chest ache, a pain of longing cracking open deep inside him. He reached for his phone, but a call felt too insignificant to quell the ache. He stuffed a handful of notes into his coat pocket and left for the train.

He devoured the notes on the way to Kazuki's shop, each one only widening the chasm inside him a little more. He wanted to be angry. He wanted to be able to forget about Kazuki, but he exposed the cracks in Yuuki's gray malaise. He ached to return to Kazuki.

He'd always wanted to be with Kazuki.

Yuuki rushed off the train and ran the short distance to Kazuki's shop. Yuuki clutched the letters in his pocket as if they'd disappear if he stopped touching them.

He pulled on Kazuki's shop door, but it was locked. It

had only been closed for an hour, and Yuuki doubted Kazuki was really gone.

"Hello! Kazuki!" Yuuki banged on the door. "I need to see you."

A woman with short hair came to the door. She pointed to the sign and mouthed that they were closed, but Yuuki banged louder.

Her eyes narrowed, but she opened the door. "We're not—"

Yuuki forced his way across the threshold and strode toward the back. "Kazuki!"

Kazuki stood there ironing pieces of a suit. He set the iron in its holster. It gurgled and a cloud of steam erupted.

He wiped a thin layer of sweat from his brow with his rolled-up sleeve. Fine strands of his long hair clung to the side of his face.

"How can I help you?" he asked. His chipper tone failed to hide his exhaustion.

"Why?" Yuuki held up a note, not trusting his voice to say anything more.

"I always cherished them, but I have no right to keep them. Not anymore. Throwing them away felt wrong. I'm sorry if I simply passed the burden on to you. But…" Kazuki bit his lip. "I never stopped loving you."

Yuuki's muscles tightened as if bracing himself for another punch, but the needling ache pulsing inside him for so long finally stopped. The chasm inside him filled.

"No man has ever come close to the way I felt when I was with you," Yuuki confessed.

Another puff of steam left the iron, and Yuuki stepped close to grasp Kazuki's hands in his.

"Let's see if we were better left as a memory," Yuuki said.

Kazuki razed a brow. "If that's your way of asking me on a date, it's not going to work."

"Would you like to go on a date?"

Kazuki's smile warmed Yuuki's heart. The smile was different from the one in his memories. Better.

"We can watch the Tigers playoff game," Yuuki suggested.

"I'd like that."

"You won't change your mind?"

Yuuki leaned in for a kiss. Their lips met, and Kazuki's mouth parted, deepening the kiss. Yuuki squeezed Kazuki's hand tighter, worried if he let go, Kazuki would disappear. Yuuki would never forget the way it felt slipping back into Kazuki's arms. It was like discovering a beloved but forgotten coat still fit.

"Does that put your mind at ease?" Yuuki asked.

"Yes, it does."

# chapter 14

*October 31*

Kazuki tapped his thumb along the edge of his beer glass. The condensation pooled, and a long tear rolled down to the warped paper coaster. He'd arrived at the small bar early enough to grab one of the three booths. He'd picked the one with the best view, but with huge screens dominating the small bar, it was hard to miss the game from any angle.

He gulped down the last of his beer and glanced at the hanging Tigers pennants. He wouldn't look at his watch. Not again. Not after the last time he'd looked and only three minutes had passed.

The alcohol sloshed in his stomach like a ship on the sea. Yuuki would come. He'd been the one to ask Kazuki out in the first place.

"Hey." Yuuki slid into the booth.

He took off his coat, exposing a Tigers jersey and slacks, but it looked good on him. Showing off his muscled arms and the casual way his hair flipped to the side. His contacts had been replaced by black-framed glasses.

Yuuki's eyes moved up and down Kazuki's attire. "I feel underdressed."

"Habit."

"Well, consider me impressed. You made it?"

Kazuki nodded, too worried he'd get too tongue-tied to say something coherent. In reality, all the late dinners of fatty eel had caused his casual clothes to look awful on him, so he'd gone with blue tartan pants, a matching vest, and a button-down from his work wardrobe.

Kazuki grabbed the bartender's attention and ordered them both a round of drinks.

"You picked a place close to my home on purpose?" Yuuki asked.

"Less chance you'd change your mind." Kazuki rubbed his neck. "Even after that kiss, I was worried you'd change your mind."

Yuuki laughed. "What happened to that confidence you oozed during high school?"

"Come on, you know when it came to you, that confidence went out the window."

"Let's not spend this whole evening going down memory lane. Let's actually get to know each other as we are now."

"I'd like that."

But before their conversation could get going, the bar erupted in cheers and chants for the team. Of course, no talking could happen when the Tigers were up to bat. So Kazuki's gaze bounced between the game and Yuuki watching the game.

Even though they couldn't talk through the drinks and shared enjoyment of the game, all the awkwardness slipped away.

When the teams switched off and the murmur of chatter between the groups gathered in the bar faded, Kazuki broke the silence between them.

"So do you have any pets?" Kazuki asked since it was a good starter question.

"My mom has five Pomeranians. Visiting them is enough pet exposure for me."

"Five is a lot."

"She gets them because I don't give her grandchildren."

Kazuki laughed, but when Yuuki didn't join Kazuki, his muscles tightened. "You're serious?"

"How did you go from astronomy to suits?" Yuuki asked, completely changing topics.

"You knew my dad was a tailor, and Hana was brought up expecting to be a designer." Kazuki shrugged. "Her father made me spend some time in every part of their business. After the divorce, I spent about a year learning at a Tokyo suit shop but moved back to open my own shop."

"What made you want to come back? We'd always talked about moving to Tokyo."

"It's expensive. Not to mention they already had enough bespoke suit ateliers. Kyoto feels like home, and it felt right to open the shop here."

"What was Tokyo like?"

"Because it's so big, there's a good amount of anonymity, but that got tiring after a while. A lot more gay bars, but Kyoto pulled me back."

Yuuki propped his head up with his hand, his elbow resting on the tabletop. "Tell me more."

Kazuki went on talking about the variety of food and how hard it was to find an apartment in his price range. What he thought was boring, lit up Yuuki's eyes, and he'd ask Kazuki to go on.

Yuuki sighed, pushing his empty beer glass back and forth between his hands. "It would be nice to live outside Kyoto, even for a few years."

"What's stopping you?"

"There's a lot of politics involved if I move."

Kazuki raised a brow, but the crowd began to cheer again as the Tigers came up to bat.

Their conversation paused for the game, but it didn't stop their connection. The alcohol flowed and enhanced their experience. They talked on and off for three hours until the Tigers lost the game. Even then, despite his favorite team's loss, Yuuki's smile couldn't have been wider.

"Do you want to go for a walk or something?" Kazuki asked.

"We can't go to a love hotel—"

"I wasn't talking about that."

Yuuki grinned. "We'll have to go back to my place, but the walls are thin. All the close love hotels are owned by the family I work for."

"Oh." Kazuki's cheeks grew hot, and he bit the inside of his cheek.

"If that's what you want."

"It's just been a while."

"Then I'll make sure it's good."

They stumbled out of the bar into the late October chill. With Yuuki beside him, Kazuki couldn't feel the cold. Everything glowed, and whether it was from the alcohol or the tingling of renewed romance, Kazuki couldn't tell.

"I can't believe they lost." Yuuki shook his head.

"The Tigers almost had it."

"They were having such a good season." Yuuki mumbled something about betting and pineapples that Kazuki didn't ask about.

They turned the corner into a neighborhood of small apartment complexes with newer houses between. People walked their dogs and ran along the sidewalk.

The yipping of a small dog stopped Yuuki. Kazuki followed his gaze to an elderly woman with a small pack of dogs. The dogs barked and charged toward Yuuki. The woman looked too frail to hold them back.

"Is that your mom? She looks… different." Kazuki bit his lip.

"She's been sick."

"Oh, I didn't—"

"It's fine. She might not remember you, or she might seem a little off."

The little dogs greeted them first. Yuuki crouched down and petted each of the yappy dogs. Yuuki's mom looked thin, too thin.

Yuuki stood. "You should really be wearing a heavier coat with how cold it's getting."

"I'll be fine. It was a quick run to the park." Even her voice sounded forty years older than it should've been. "It's nice to see you smiling."

Yuuki's cheeks reddened. "Mom, you remember Kazuki from when I was in high school?"

"My hair was a lot shorter back then," Kazuki said.

She tilted her head, but then her eyes widened. "Your wedding was one of the most beautiful I've attended." She squeezed Kazuki's hands. Her sickly thin hands left an unshakable chill in him. "The kimonos everyone wore were so pretty."

"Oh, yes."

"Yuuki had some kind of stomach bug and spent the whole ceremony in the bathroom."

"Mom!" Yuuki said.

Kazuki laughed. "Honestly, he didn't miss much."

"It's nice to see you two getting along again." She leaned closer to Kazuki. "Yuuki was really devastated when that invitation came in the mail."

"Mother!"

She turned toward Yuuki. "I haven't been able to find the usual dog treats at the store, and Peaches doesn't like the brand I got."

"It's the dark blue box, remember?"

"I couldn't find it."

"I'll get some next time I'm at the store. You really shouldn't be out in the cold for so long."

She waved off his warning, then she and her pack of dogs drifted the opposite way. Yuuki shoved his hands into his pockets and walked ahead a few paces.

Yuuki sighed. "I moved closer to her last year so I could be there when she needed me. Now I run into her on the street every few days."

Kazuki laughed. "No wonder you're so popular with her dogs."

"Anyone willing to give them a pat on the head is popular with them."

Yuuki's apartment was in a simple building holding under thirty units. Everything looked neat and orderly just like the minutes Yuuki used to take during student council meetings.

"It's a nice place," Kazuki said.

"I would've wanted a separate bedroom, but it was the only one available at the time."

Yuuki sat on the bed with Kazuki joining him. Their fingers were interlaced, and Kazuki never wanted to let go.

"Moving and taking care of your mom must've been difficult," Kazuki said.

"I don't know." Yuuki sighed. "Sometimes I just feel numb to it altogether."

"I shouldn't have brought it up."

Yuuki looked off into the distance, but he squeezed Kazuki's hand tighter.

"They gave her six months."

"I'm so sorry."

"That was a year ago." Yuuki's Adam's apple bobbed. "You don't know how strange it is. Of course, the doctor didn't tell her that, so I kept it to myself. Four months came, then five. I prepared myself, but the end didn't come. Every day I would enter her apartment thinking it would be the day, but it hasn't come yet. I know I should be happy, but I don't know how to get back there. And what if tomorrow is the last day?"

"Yuuki…"

Kazuki's heart screamed, and he pulled Yuuki close. The hug would never be close enough. Kazuki couldn't tell if the embrace was for Yuuki or him.

"Thank you," Kazuki said. "Thank you for telling me."

Yuuki rubbed his eyes. "I must be drunk because I haven't told anyone that before."

"We can drink some more and forget the whole thing if you want."

His fingers wrapped around Kazuki's long hair and gave it a tug. Yuuki's lips burned against Kazuki's, and the heat between them ignited. Yuuki knew exactly where to stick his tongue and press his lips to send the room spinning.

"I've wanted to run my fingers through your hair from the moment I saw you in the shop," Yuuki whispered into Kazuki's ear before kissing down his neck.

Yuuki pushed Kazuki onto the bed and climbed on top. Their kiss deepened, but then Yuuki's phone rang. Kazuki ignored it, but Yuuki pulled away. He stretched his neck to see who was calling.

"It's Jun. I have to answer." Yuuki grabbed his phone and answered.

"Nothing serious," Jun said. "But the Ukyo ward ran out of candy to give out for Halloween. Go get them some."

"Of course. I'll get right on it."

Yuuki hung up and squeezed his hand into fists.

"Sorry, but I have to go," Yuuki said.

"To deliver candy?"

"I know it's stupid."

"Then can't you send someone else?"

"I can't. My boss asked *me* to do it." Yuuki rubbed the bridge of his nose. "That makes it sound worse, doesn't it? And here I was hoping I could tell you after mind-blowing sex. I'm a yakuza."

Kazuki laughed.

Yuuki's eyes narrowed. "I am being serious. I've been one since I graduated from high school. What? You don't believe I could be a gangster?"

"I knew you were a yakuza when you poured that whiskey for Jun."

"And you don't mind?"

"You're still Yuuki, and I still want to know who you are now."

Yuuki smiled and gyrated his hips against Kazuki's "All my exes dumped me once they found out."

"Then I'm better than your exes."

Yuuki pulled Kazuki into another kiss, silencing his words. "I'll make this up to you, I promise. It's usually not as simple as candy."

"So we'll have another date?"

"Definitely, and I promise it will be even better."

# chapter 15

*November 1*

Yuuki's wishful thinking that he could return home after delivering the candy vanished when Jun asked him to stay for the festivities.

The ward had gone all out, building a three-room haunted house and a place for parents to take photos with their children. The optics would be good for the family, especially with the bloodbath the summer turf war had caused. Still, the celebration was Western and something their godfather would forbid, which was why they'd brought Jun.

Yuuki tossed the last of the candy bars to a straggling teenager who'd stayed out late.

"You wanna head to the club?" Jun asked. The white-blue vampire makeup he'd worn had faded and cracked into the wrinkles around his eyes.

Jun always asked, which was polite, but Yuuki doubted Jun would really enjoy his company.

"I'm worn out." Yuuki faked a yawn. "But I can drive you to the club if you'd like."

"I'll have one of these guys take me." Jun turned to chat up a local guy.

Yuuki left the ward a little before eleven. His heart ached, and his fingers longed to be interlaced with Kazuki's. It wasn't too late, and Yuuki hadn't planned on going to bed alone.

*Want a late-night snack?* he texted Kazuki. It seemed playful enough.

Two train stops later, Kazuki texted back. *I'll take a Kit Kat. Meet me at the back of the shop.*

Yuuki's eyes narrowed. It wasn't the sexy reply he'd expected, but Kazuki could've pretended to be asleep. So Yuuki stopped at a convenience store for the second time that night.

The back door of Kazuki's shop had been propped open with a brick. Yuuki slipped inside, but Kazuki wasn't anywhere in the storage room. Yuuki pressed forward, finding Kazuki in the sewing room hunched over a table and chalking lines on fabric.

Kazuki's precise and agile movements demonstrated his skill. His fingers glanced over the fabric, his long hair dripping over his shoulder. Yuuki swallowed and took a step closer.

Kazuki jumped, grabbing his chest. "You scared me."

"I thought the open door meant you wanted me to come in."

"I did, but you could have made a bit of noise."

"I'll remember that for next time." Yuuki reached into the bag and grabbed a random Kit Kat. "I wasn't sure what flavor you wanted, so I got a few different types."

"How many did you get?"

"A few." Yuuki opened the bag. "A dozen. Maybe two."

Kazuki laughed. "That's more than a few."

"Passing out so much candy made me want to have some for us to enjoy."

Kazuki reached into the bag and selected one from the

bunch. "I'll save this one as good luck for the fashion show I have in February."

"Four months is a long way off."

Kazuki held up the candy. "And I'm running behind and need all the luck I can get."

"Maybe you need to take two."

"And then what do we do with the others?"

Yuuki jiggled the bag. "Late-night snack?"

"Okay, but we need to eat in the office. I don't want any chocolate getting on the fabric." Kazuki headed to the room Yuuki had entered through.

"Wait, that's an office? I thought it was storage."

"Only part of it is a storage room. I've been too busy to clean it up."

Yuuki fought the urge to organize the stacks of papers Kazuki moved around to give him enough room to lean against the desk and Yuuki enough room to sit.

They unwrapped the first of their treats—green tea flavored. A perfect starter before some of the limited-edition flavor combinations Yuuki had grabbed.

The long Kit Kat sticks pressed against Kazuki's lush lips, teasing Yuuki. He licked his lips, then leaned forward, getting a little closer. A tingling heat coursed through Yuuki.

"Is the fashion show open to the public?" he asked.

"There's limited seating."

"Oh…" Yuuki ripped open the newest pack, purple potato, and held up two sticks for Kazuki. "They record it, then?"

Kazuki's eyes widened. "You'd actually want to go?"

"To support you? Sure."

"You won't be bored out of your mind and pissed Hana's helping me?"

"Why would I care about your ex-wife now?" Yuuki ran

his hand along Kazuki's inner thigh. "It's clear I won in the end."

Kazuki frowned.

"I'm joking." Yuuki stood and nipped at Kazuki's neck. "We have time for a quickie before it gets too late."

"It's not that easy for me."

Yuuki palmed Kazuki's crotch. "You're getting excited already."

Kazuki pushed Yuuki's hand away.

"I'm infertile."

"Good, then I don't have to worry about getting pregnant." Yuuki laughed.

It was a joke. It was meant to be a joke, but Kazuki's face sank, and the pain in his eyes pierced Yuuki's heart.

Yuuki pressed his lips together. "I'm sorry—"

"You wouldn't joke if you had to live through it." Kazuki's words stung.

"Then tell me about it."

"You wouldn't want to know."

"Try me."

Kazuki's sigh spoke of his doubt, but Yuuki squeezed his hands.

"I mean it," Yuuki said. "Talking about your lack of pets or the Tigers game isn't really going to get us caught up with who we are now. I want to know."

"Going into the marriage with Hana, I knew we were going to have children," Kazuki said. "My father-in-law pulled me aside after the wedding and told me about the long family history, telling me the sooner it continued the better.

"So we never worried about birth control. We went through college together, and after a while, we deiced to really try, but after a year, nothing happened. I didn't think much about it, figuring it would happen at some point, but

Hana went to a fertility clinic without me knowing. It went downhill from there." Kazuki closed his eyes. "Are you sure you want all the details?"

The heaviness in Kazuki's voice didn't escape Yuuki's notice.

"Don't push yourself if you're not ready."

Kazuki hung his head, his hair covering his eyes. "I haven't talked about it before."

Yuuki squeezed Kazuki's hand once more. "Then I'll wait until you're ready."

They sat in silence for a few more minutes before Kazuki spoke again. "Sex wasn't spontaneous anymore. The end goal was a theoretical child. I felt more like a walking sperm donor. Sex was a chore. I stopped feeling attractive. Eventually, Hana made me go to the doctor myself, and it turned out I was sterile.

"There were things to help, but I hadn't been happy with our relationship for a long time. With the fertility results, I finally found a way out of our marriage, and we divorced."

"Don't worry. I don't want you for your sperm," Yuuki said.

Kazuki laughed. "I'm glad."

"Can you tell me how you make a suit? You looked hot with that chalk."

"Oh, yes, chalk dust is very sexy."

# chapter 16

*November 14*

Two weeks had passed since Kazuki and Yuuki's first date, and in the time since, they threaded their lives together as easily as twine.

Allowing Yuuki to become his muse, Kazuki's creativity flowed. His sketchbook became filled with more pictures of Yuuki, but more importantly, the sketches were of Yuuki wearing suits.

"It has to be here somewhere." Kazuki pushed aside the long boxes of the newly arrived fabric.

Shizuri stepped over one of the paper stacks and began steeping some green tea in two mugs. "You should organize this mess at some point."

"It's not a mess. This room is small, so it looks cluttered. I know exactly where everything is."

Her upturned lip spoke of her doubt.

"I do," Kazuki lied, flipping through another stack in search of the document verifying his original fabric order from the supplier.

"You could always pay someone to help. There are lots of organizations that help hoarders."

"I'm not that bad! Once things slow down, I'll create a new system."

"And when will that be?" She pulled the sachets of tea leaves from the cups and tossed them in the trash.

"After the fashion show."

"When we get a rush of new clients?"

Kazuki let out a little laugh. "When we move into a bigger shop?"

"I can already see you shoving everything into boxes and never unpacking."

"They'd be organized boxes."

She laughed, her tone lighthearted for the first time Kazuki could remember.

"We'll finish up today's work before the tea gets cold." She grabbed the mugs in one hand.

"That's quick."

"It helps having another set of hands. Though I miss the eel dinners. You could always order it for us as a thank-you."

"I've had enough eel dinners for a lifetime."

"Impossible. You can never have too much eel."

Shizuri slipped back into the sewing room.

The new sewer had started a little over a week ago, and with the extra set of hands, they'd finally put a dent in the mountain of orders. If only they could find someone who didn't shake with terror when a yakuza entered the store, then Kazuki wouldn't have to take a break from cutting fabric to take measurements.

A knock sounded on the back door, and Kazuki's heart thudded with anticipation. He opened the door, his lips connecting with Yuuki's before he could take a step inside. His warm lips mixed with the November cold sent a tickle down

Kazuki's spine. He'd never felt more alone than during the two nights Yuuki had just spent in Hokkaido.

"I missed you," Kazuki said.

Yuuki's arms wrapped around Kazuki's waist. "I missed you, too, but it'll only be a few more months that I'll have to travel."

"How was Hokkaido?"

"Cold. I'm glad to be home. I'm glad to be here with you." Yuuki tugged off his leather gloves and shoved them into his coat pocket. "You've reorganized."

"I had to make room when the fashion show fabric was delivered."

Yuuki remained a foot inside the room, the only space free from the organized paper stacks. A little thread pulled at Kazuki's heart as he took in Yuuki's stiff pose and thin lips. Could he really be so uncomfortable with the cluttered space, or was something else going on?

"How did the fabric from the new supplier turn out?" Yuuki asked.

"I wanted to open it with you."

Yuuki's smile could've warmed Kazuki on even the most frigid day. "You didn't have to wait for me."

"I wanted to. Especially since you're my muse for this collection."

Yuuki's cheeks turned the cutest shade of pink.

Even though their rekindled relationship was new, the only days they hadn't seen each other were the two days Yuuki had spent in Hokkaido. They'd fallen into a rhythm as easily as picking up an old sewing project.

Yuuki would come over a little after the shop closed. He would tap away at some program on his laptop while Kazuki cut out the suit for the next day's sewing. Their light chatter filled the air, and the hours slipped by without them even noticing until their stomachs grumbled. A late dinner together was usually followed by an intimate night at Kazuki's apartment.

During Yuuki's absence, the void in Kazuki's bed traveled into the store. It had built into a tearing longing that had stunned Kazuki because it had happened so soon, but then again, it hadn't. The longing had been there since their breakup in high school. Kazuki never wanted to let go again.

Yuuki slid off his coat, and Kazuki took it. The coat didn't hug the lines of Yuuki's body well enough for Kazuki's liking. He'd already made a note somewhere to snatch it out of Yuuki's closet when the seasons changed.

Kazuki hung the coat next to his, then turned. His gaze locked on the dark-brown spattered stains on Yuuki's white shirt.

"What's wrong?" Yuuki followed Kazuki's gaze. "Oh."

Kazuki swallowed. "That's blood, isn't it?"

Yuuki didn't speak, but he didn't have to. His shoulders slumped, and he turned as if begging Kazuki not to look.

"It is, isn't it?"

"Don't worry about it. It's nothing."

Yuuki's words made a pincushion out of Kazuki's heart.

Kazuki wasn't dating a more mature version of high-school Yuuki. This Yuuki jumped to answer a call from his boss, no matter the situation. This Yuuki casually dismissed bloodstains like they were lint. This Yuuki was a yakuza.

"T-tell me." Kazuki hated the way his voice shook.

Yuuki's gaze moved to the other side of the room, then slowly back to Kazuki. His eyes weren't cold or piercing. They were the same honey-brown Kazuki had always known, and it felt like Yuuki was about to quote some math theorem Kazuki needed for his exam practice. Something about that twisted Kazuki's every fiber.

"I want to know!" Kazuki pushed.

Yuuki sighed. It was a long sigh filled with impending resignation. "Jun and I were looking into a disturbance, and while we were there, someone threw a brick through the window."

"Are you okay?"

"It's not my blood."

Kazuki's legs went weak. He leaned against his desk for support.

Yuuki's lips pressed into a thin line. "If you don't want to know, then why did you ask?"

"Because normal people ask about blood when they see it on their boyfriend's shirt."

Yuuki popped the top button of his collared shirt free.

"Do you seriously think this is turning me on?"

"I'm trying to take this shirt off. Unless you'd rather I go home and we forget—" Yuuki's phone rang, cutting off his caustic words.

Kazuki's breath caught in his throat. No doubt the call would be Jun, sending Yuuki off on a mission, but instead of being something silly like delivering candy, it would be to kill.

"It's my mom," Yuuki said. "I need to make sure she's okay." He clicked the button and turned. "Hello?"

"What brand were the dog treats Tiny liked again?"

Kazuki heard Yuuki's mom's shaking words on the other end of the line. She sounded weaker than when he'd last heard her.

Yuuki rubbed his temple. "The ones in the dark blue package."

"Oh, that's right. I ran out, and I figured I'd get some at the store, but I couldn't remember the brand."

"Are you at the store now? The groceries are too heavy for you, and you'll get lost like last time."

"You worry too much. I'll be fine."

"Just go home and write the list, and I'll get everything tomorrow. The dogs can live without treats for one night."

"Do you think they'll have any good ginkgo nuts?"

"Just write it on the list."

"How about—

Yuuki squeezed his eyes shut as if in pain. "Mom, I gotta go. I'm in the middle of something."

"Oh, you were in the middle of a date, weren't you?"

"Sure."

"I knew it," she said. "You've been so happy lately. I knew it had to be because you're dating someone you really like."

"I'll come by tomorrow. Call a taxi and go home."

"I walked here. I'll be fine walking back."

"I don't want you to get lost again."

"You worry too much."

"Please."

Kazuki felt the pain in Yuuki's words as he desperately pleaded with his mother. It hurt. The sudden switch of emotion from anger to pity was jarring. Yuuki had so much more going on in his life than Kazuki could ever know.

"Sorry about that," Yuuki said. "I'll be going. If you don't want me to come back here let me know."

"Wait." Kazuki grabbed Yuuki's shirt. The blood-stained fabric wrinkled underneath his fingers. "White vinegar should get the blood stains out. We have some here."

"You want me to stay?" Yuuki asked, doubt saturating his words.

Kazuki stood on wobbly legs but began to unbutton Yuuki's shirt. "Letting you go so soon after I've only just gotten to know who you are now would be a decision I would regret for the rest of my life."

"Hmm."

Kazuki tugged Yuuki's shirt off and found the vinegar underneath the sink.

"Thanks." Yuuki's voice was small.

Kazuki laughed. "The first time I accidentally nicked my finger, Shizuri insisted we keep a big bottle of the stuff."

"You are still the most absent-minded person I know."

The simple back and forth helped lighten the mood in the room, but it didn't completely deflate the tension as Kazuki blotted the stains over the sink.

"It must be hard, having to take care of your mom like that," Kazuki said.

"She gets a checkup soon. I don't know if I want to know the results or not anymore."

"Do you want me to go with you? It might be nice to have company there."

"She might get suspicious." Yuuki wrung his hands together. "Have you come out to your parents? Being bi, you probably haven't bothered."

"No, I told them."

"How did it go?"

"I told them when I told them about the divorce. I figured getting everything out at once would be easier. They disowned me, and I haven't talked to them since."

Yuuki's eyes went wide. "Really? Not even a New Year's visit?"

"You know how my parents were." Kazuki scrubbed a stubborn stain a little harder. "Are you thinking of telling your mom?"

"It never felt worth the risk."

"I think it will be different with your mother." Kazuki cracked a smile. "I mean, I'm sure your aunt knows. Remember how she'd always knock and wait for us to answer the door before coming in."

"That's because her hands were usually full of food for us."
Kazuki shrugged. "I think this stain needs to soak more."

"Should we open the fabric boxes, then?"

"Yeah, I want to know what you think." Kazuki went digging through his desk for his nonfabric scissors but then heard a click. His attention snapped to the sound, and he saw Yuuki sliding a knife along the taped box.

The unsettling tension stirring inside Kazuki evaporated when Yuuki pulled out the most colorful fabric Kazuki could imagine. The small samples Hana had given him were nothing compared to how the colors popped in person.

Yuuki held it up. Without the collared shirt and black jacket, he looked like any man in an undershirt. But more importantly, the fabric against his skin looked like the last thing a yakuza would wear.

"It's so colorful," Yuuki said.

"It's perfect for the spring season. Do you like it?"
Yuuki nodded. "I do."

Kazuki squeezed Yuuki's hand before giving Yuuki a hesitant kiss. A small moan escaped from the back of Yuuki's throat. He opened his mouth but waited for Kazuki to dominate the kiss. The tenderness set all of Kazuki's conflicted feelings free. Two weeks was too soon to put an end to a relationship that made him feel *this* good.

Breathless, Kazuki pulled away. "I want to make you a closet filled with suits made from these fabrics."

Yuuki laughed. "I'd like that."

# *chapter 17*



*December 1*

Yuuki hated how used to the grind of hospitals he'd become. The long waits, the multiple people in and out before things seemed to actually happen. The checkups weren't so bad, but Yuuki and his mom had only been to a few so far.

The odd blue walls of the examination room did little to calm Yuuki. The 3D brain model only conjured up memories of the doctor pointing out sections where the cancer had already ravaged his mother's brain. Yuuki looked away, but there was no way to escape the macabre medical posters. He clutched his journal a little tighter, knowing from experience that when his mother was wheeled in for her brain scan, he could pour every fear and hope into its pages and maintain the neutral exterior his mother needed.

"When do I get to meet your mystery date?" Mom asked.

"What?"

Mom smiled, perched on the examination table, wearing

a hospital gown. "You've been so happy lately. It must be because you're in love."

Yuuki's cheeks grew hot. "Not necessarily. It's been nice to see Aunt Miko regularly. I've missed having her around."

She tapped her head. "I'm still here enough to know you wouldn't have that light back in your eyes because you can see Miko."

Yuuki licked his lips. It must've been true. Things had seemed easier than they used to feel, but it wasn't like the melancholic cloud that usually hung over his head had faded completely. It was still hovering off in the distance.

"Mom…"

A knock on the door was quickly followed by the doctor's entrance. Yuuki's eyes widened. It wasn't his mother's usual doctor.

"Dr. Ito called in sick today, but I've stepped in to help with his cases. I'm Dr. Sara Yamamoto, a fellow brain surgeon, and I will be looking after you today." Her eyes widened as her gaze met Yuuki's.

Their schedules hadn't matched up enough for Yuuki to come see Sara's home or work out when they'd announce the wedding to their parents. It might've been because all the dates Sara had available, had been dates Yuuki had already planned to see Kazuki. Every night he wasn't in Hokkaido, he'd been with Kazuki.

"You're a woman," Mom said.

"I can assure you the only difference between me and Dr. Ito is his age in terms of experience," Sara said.

"And maybe twenty kilos." Mom laughed. "I think it's amazing. It would be helpful if there were more women doctors. It would put my mind at ease."

Sara remained professional, running through the usual list of questions the doctors asked. Yuuki knew the drill—some questions asked and answered, then Mom would be wheeled away, and the doctor would expect the real answers from him. Then he'd be left alone for what felt like hours until the scan was finished and the doctor could look at the results.

When the questions for his mom were finished, Sara called in a nurse to wheel Mom away.

"It's going to get awkward if we don't tell her we're dating," Sara said.

"I know."

"Now would be the perfect time to get the marriage announcement out of the way."

Yuuki pressed his lips together. Somehow even a fake marriage didn't sit well with him anymore.

"I'm going to have to back out," Yuuki said. "I found a really amazing guy, and—

"Like I said, I don't care if you date as long as you keep up the sham when my parents visit."

"I know."

Yet the days Yuuki had been in Hokkaido had been the loneliest he could remember. If had a choice, he wouldn't go. He wanted to spend every night with Kazuki.

"We can announce it when she's finished with the scan."

"I can't. I'm sorry if it felt like I was leading you on. I didn't mean to. I wish you the best in your search."

—

*December 17*

A better secretary would've been taking notes during Jun's meeting with Kurosawa, but Yuuki couldn't find the need to.

The negotiations with the Hokkaido mafia had been going smoothly. Jun could schmooze any sucker.

So as the meeting droned on and there was nothing for Yuuki to directly concern himself with, he lived in his memories. Instead of going out for dinner, Kazuki had made a quiet meal at home. His cooking skills hadn't improved since their high school's cultural fair, but Yuuki's yakuza recruit training saved the nikujaga from becoming too much of a disaster. The meat and potato stew had been perfect for the chilly weather.

After dinner, they'd spent the night together like all the other nights, but instead of passionate lovemaking, they'd lain in bed gazing into each other's eyes and talking about their future together. Kazuki's hair twisted in Yuuki's fingers. He never wanted the night to end.

"Yuuki!" Jun's sharp tone stabbed through the memory.

Yuuki cleared his throat. "Sorry, I missed that."

"The Hokkaido mafia mentioned something about eyeball technology. You know what they're talking about."

"I spoke with their director, Shinji, about how if he had the data about where people watched, he could make sure to get the shots. You can track where people look during the videos."

"Now they want eyeball tracking technology as part of the alliance package."

"There's publicly available software. It would be hard to find volunteers to watch porn."

"All this new technology." Kurosawa rubbed his wrinkled forehead. "Let's simply offer them free use of the film sets we have here."

Jun tapped the ash off his cigarette. "I'll say that is a better deal. Right now, our target for the formal sake exchange is February eleventh."

Yuuki's breath caught in the back of his throat. February

eleventh was the day of Kazuki's fashion show. Not only had he promised Kazuki he'd be there, but Yuuki wanted to be.

"Is it such a good idea to have it in the middle of the week like that?" Yuuki asked.

Kurosawa and Jun both turned to glare at him. Yuuki gulped and sank deeper into his chair. He never spoke up at meetings unless specifically asked a question, let alone dare to disagree.

"National Foundation Day is an auspicious occasion." Jun's pointed tone dared Yuuki to open his mouth again.

"Of course, I apologize," Yuuki said.

——

*January 4*

Yuuki did everything he could to make the blow of breaking his promise to Kazuki hurt less. Kazuki was out of his office, finalizing the fashion show designs with Hana and seeing her new baby, so with Shizuri's help, they were able to tackle the project that had been on Kazuki's to-do list for months.

Yuuki hid behind the desk. His stomach was knotted twine. The door to the office swung open.

Yuuki jumped up. "Surprise!"

Kazuki's eyes widened, he dropped his bag, and Yuuki couldn't tell if his open mouth was happy surprise or anger.

"Where did all my papers go?" Kazuki asked.

Everything from the tea containers to the extra fabric stash had been organized, labeled, and properly filed for ease of use. Yuuki doubted it would fully make up for missing the fashion show—it probably wouldn't make up for missing the fashion show at all—but Yuuki hoped Kazuki would feel his love through his actions.

The corners of Kazuki's lips turned up in a wide smile. His arms wrapped around Yuuki, squeezing out the last bit of Yuuki's doubts.

"I can't believe you would do something like this." Kazuki's whispered breath tickled Yuuki's ear.

Kazuki pulled away.

The cold breeze Kazuki had brought in with him raised goose bumps over Yuuki's skin. He squeezed his lover's hands, keeping the warmth of reuniting between them for a few extra seconds.

"Shizuri told me you are looking into hiring someone to help you organize." Yuuki shrugged. "Why bother hiring someone when I could do it for you? You could've asked me ages ago."

"I wouldn't want to ask you to do something so boring." Kazuki's callused fingertips trailed down Yuuki's palm.

"That's what being in a relationship is about, sharing the boring parts of life because together, they're a little more interesting."

Kazuki's hands slipped away, and he opened the new filing cabinet in the corner.

"You put dividers in and everything," Kazuki said.

"It gets better." Yuuki ushered Kazuki into the computer chair. "Click on your store logo."

Kazuki clicked on the new tree icon.

With one click, the past two weeks of work came to a head. With the short timeline, Yuuki hadn't been able to get all the features he wanted programmed, but for a user-friendly, searchable database it did what he wanted.

"If you click here and type in a client's name." Yuuki stood behind Kazuki and typed in Murata giving a list of a few names. He clicked on Father Murata's name. "You have all the suits he's ever ordered, fabric selections, and measurements. You can even write notes."

"You did this with everyone?" Kazuki asked.

"Text reading software made it easy to scan. I left the software on the computer. If you want to keep the paper system you can, but with the database, it will be easier to find things."

"This will make everything so much faster."

"It's not exactly the prettiest software."

"Who cares. I won't have to memorize what I put in what stack."

Yuuki chuckled. "And I can walk without worrying about knocking one of the stacks over."

Kazuki leaned back in his chair and met Yuuki's gaze above him. Kazuki's eyes were a beautiful golden brown.

"This is the most thoughtful thing someone has done for me in a long time," Kazuki said.

"It was noth—"

Kazuki tugged on Yuuki's shirt collar, pulling him into a kiss, tender but burning and stained with the bitterness of what Yuuki needed to say. He could easily get lost in the heat. He opened his mouth wider and tangled his fingers in Kazuki's hair. It took everything for Yuuki not to simply come around and straddle Kazuki's lap.

Yuuki opened his eyes and pulled out of Kazuki's reach. "There's something I have to say."

"I love you too," Kazuki breathed out. "Now kiss me again so we can get to sex on the floor."

Yuuki swallowed. Pinpricks snaked along his neck then twisted into a tourniquet in his stomach.

Kazuki blinked, and the euphoric light in his eyes dimmed. They'd confessed their love countless times in the past, but they hadn't uttered the words recently.

Yuuki's stomach quivered, from nausea or nerves he couldn't tell. He swallowed, grabbing a lock of Kazuki's hair and kissing the strand.

"I love you too." The tourniquet twisting in Yuuki's stomach loosened. "That's why it's so hard for me to tell you I won't be able to make it to your fashion show. I know, I promised I would go, and I want to go, but there's this huge thing at work happening, and I have to be there."

"You make it sound like you're never coming back." Kazuki's eyes grew wide. "Wait, you are coming back?"

"Of course I'm coming back. Why would you think I wouldn't?"

"Well… with your profession."

Yuuki sighed.

"You look so upset," Kazuki said.

Yuuki dug his knuckles into his thigh. "I was excited to go to your show. I was with you when you opened the fabric and when you did the sketches. I wanted to be there for you from start to finish."

"I can get someone to record it."

"It won't be the same, but it's as close as I'll get."

Kazuki laughed tugging Yuuki onto his lap. "You're more upset about this than I am. Don't beat yourself up about it."

Yuuki looked away but twirled the lock of Kazuki's hair around his finger. "I hate how I don't have any kind of say in my life."

"It sounds like you don't want to be a yakuza anymore."

"I never wanted to be one in the first place."

"Then leave." Kazuki shrugged. "I know a dozen businesses who would buy up that program you built for me. If you don't want to do that, then I could always use extra help around the shop. I won't mind if your pinkie is missing."

Yuuki laughed. "Cutting off pinkies is old-fashioned. Most just have you shave your head now."

"Well, then it's good your hair isn't as long as mine."

"Even then, it's not as simple for me."

"Why?" Kazuki squeezed Yuuki's hand. "You always change the subject when it comes to your work. If you want to leave, I don't get why you don't just go."

Yuuki pressed his lips together. "You remember my aunt Miko?"

"The one who would knock really loudly and bring us dinner when your mother had to work late?"

"Yes." Yuuki sighed. "She's currently the head of the Kyoto mob."

"Oh… that's big."

"In high school, I had no idea. She said she was a businesswoman, and I believed her. Why wouldn't I? When she found out I failed the entrance exam and was looking into cram schools, she told me to rethink my life, that maybe I could get a degree, but any job that did a background check would see the mob connection. I'm happy you want me to work here, but I'll only bring you more yakuza clients."

Kazuki looked down for an unsettling amount of time, but he eventually met Yuuki's gaze with a smile.

"You might miss this year's fashion show, but you'll make it next year," Kazuki said.

Yuuki didn't miss the fact that Kazuki didn't bring up the mob, but he forced a smile. "You're right. There's always next year."

# chapter 18



*February 1*

The atmosphere in Kyoto changed subtly. Throughout January, it became harder and harder to ignore. First weekly, then daily, news reports told of various horrors sweeping the city, everything from graffiti to arson. Each new report sent a pulse of dread through Kazuki's bones.

Yuuki never mentioned what was going on, not that Kazuki would ask. He'd learned long ago that it was better to ignore Yuuki's yakuza connection and pretend he was only a secretary to some eccentric club owner than to acknowledge it.

But it was getting harder to avoid the news and even harder to ignore Yuuki. When they touched, his muscles popped like a misaligned overlock computer. On dates, he kept looking over his shoulder so often Kazuki couldn't ignore it. Something was boiling in the Kyoto underworld, and it was too much for Kazuki to stomach.

Kazuki stepped a little closer to Yuuki on the train. While it wasn't packed, it was populated enough that standing so close wouldn't look odd.

"Thanks for today," Yuuki said, keeping his voice down so he didn't disturb the other train riders. "It really helped me get my mind off everything."

"I'm glad you enjoyed it."

They'd spent the day outside the city in a tiny village filled with tea plantations. Perhaps getting tea directly from the tree overexaggerated the whole experience, but with two weeks before the fashion show, Kazuki needed a break from the city too.

A sad smile crossed Yuuki's face before fading a second later. Kazuki swallowed, tightening his grip on the train's grip ring. Yuuki had seemed so happy at the farm.

A man in a heavy black coat staggered into the car, his face red from drink. He bounced between people and seats as he made his way down the car.

"At least we're not that drunk this time, eh?" Kazuki nodded his chin toward the stumbling man.

"It's too bad I leave for Hokkaido in the morning or else we could be."

Kazuki chuckled, clutching the handle a little tighter as the train swayed.

The drunkard bumped into Kazuki's shoulder before stumbling into the next car. Yuuki narrowed his eyes. Then his phone must have vibrated because he took it out and texted a short reply.

Kazuki's shoulders tightened, knowing what would happen next. Yuuki would excuse himself at the next stop, no doubt sent on a mission that balanced his life on a knife's edge.

The train slowed to a stop.

Yuuki stayed put as straight as a needle, but his eyes were as cold as steel.

"Is everything okay?" Kazuki dared to ask.

Yuuki sighed. "Just tired."

"There's a lot going on with work?"

"Don't worry about it."

Kazuki's skin grew hot. His heart thumped in his chest as the future grew darker than he'd dare say.

Yuuki might not be getting off the train for some mission, but it didn't stop him from doing so after he dropped Kazuki off. Sure, Yuuki was strong. He knew what he was doing, but what if one day he wasn't lucky? What if tonight was his last?

The train stopped and Yuuki and Kazuki got off. Kazuki's feet felt a little heavier, and his pace was slower.

"You okay?" Yuuki asked.

Kazuki could only nod, too worried his lips would deceive him by spilling all the struggles his heart faced. Yuuki slowed his steps to keep pace with Kazuki.

"Why don't I plan our next day since you planned this one?" Yuuki asked.

"Trading back and forth sounds fun."

Yuuki's phone buzzed. Kazuki jumped grabbing his chest.

"Aren't you going to answer it?" Kazuki asked.

"It's fine."

They arrived at Kazuki's door.

"Hope you have a good flight," Kazuki said.

"Thanks. I'll miss you, but I will be back in a few days."

With no one around, Kazuki let their goodnight kiss linger, squeezing Yuuki as tightly as he could.

Kazuki reached into his pocket to grab his keys, but his wallet was missing.

"That's odd." Kazuki patted his pockets but couldn't feel his wallet. "My wallet's gone."

"You must've dropped it at the station," Yuuki said.

"You think?"

"Someone's probably turned it in by now. I'll check lost and found and bring it back here. You go ahead and relax."

Yuuki gave Kazuki's hand a squeeze before leaving. Kazuki slipped inside his home, and once he was alone, his thoughts overflowed. It was strange that Yuuki was so sure his wallet was at the station.

Under an hour later, there was a knock at the door.

"I got your wallet back." Yuuki handed it over.

Kazuki reached out for the wallet but paused for a second. Dark marks and scratches marred Yuuki's knuckles and hands.

"Thanks." Kazuki swallowed and took the wallet, but it felt different, thicker.

"Happy to help."

"There's more money in here than there should be."

Yuuki shrugged.

"That drunk guy stole my wallet, didn't he? And you or your men found him and…"

"You want me to lie or tell the truth? What do you want me to say?"

"I—" Kazuki squeezed the wallet, but it didn't ease the knotted threads of his thoughts. He closed his eyes, and only one thought passed through his lips. "I can't deal with your yakuza life anymore. I thought it would be different. I thought I could handle the stress, but I can't."

Yuuki opened his mouth, but no words came out. The hurt in his eyes stung, but finally saying the words he had been thinking for months lifted the heavy iron on Kazuki's chest and made Kazuki feel lighter.

"I can't do this anymore." Kazuki's squeezed his eyes shut. "I'm always worried you'll get a phone call and go off to take care of whatever it is, then end up dead. I can hardly sleep anymore. Please understand—"

But when Kazuki opened his eyes again, Yuuki had already walked away.

# chapter 19



*February 4*

The icy chill of Hokkaido turned Yuuki's body numb. Usually, his thoughts of Kazuki spread a hopeful warmth through him, keeping the chill at bay, but not anymore. Yuuki knew no one wanted to date a yakuza, and he shouldn't have thought his relationship with Kazuki would turn out any differently.

Yuuki turned up his jacket's collar and strolled into the prison with the rest of the group of visitors. With less than two weeks until the planned sake exchange, Yuuki was there to get Miko's final approval.

For the first time, the guards treated Yuuki with a decent amount of respect. No doubt the local mafia showing off how much influence they had over the prison. The guard left Miko alone with him in a room that looked more doctor's office than institution. The chairs even had cushions. Yuuki didn't see any cameras in the room.

Miko greeted Yuuki by giving him a hearty hug. He sat beside her on a bright orange sofa that had to have been around for more years than he'd been alive. Miko lit up a cigarette from the pack on her wooden chair's arm.

"You're doing well?" Yuuki asked.

"Local guys proving their worth." Miko waved her hand, cigarette smoke twirling around her. "They must be asking for a fortune."

"It's pretty favorable, considering we are at their mercy."

"No one wants to get on the bad side of a demon."

Yuuki pressed his lips together. The rumors of Father Murata being a demon ready to bathe in the blood of those who crossed him helped Jun in his negotiations.

"What are their demands?" she asked.

Yuuki told his aunt everything like a good little errand boy who had no control over his life. It was his job, and no doubt it would be his job for the rest of his life. He should've burned the letters Kazuki had returned. Then at least it wouldn't hurt so much.

"How was your mother's checkup?" Miko tapped the ashes off her cigarette.

"She's still in remission."

"Then why do you look like you've just committed your first murder?"

Yuuki rubbed his neck. "I'm fine."

"Come on now." She clicked her tongue.

"It's the same stuff. Nothing to worry about."

"I doubt you'll be visiting for a while, so let me bestow one last piece of Aunt Miko wisdom on you."

Yuuki fidgeted with the zipper on his boot. Miko's pointed truth had always punctured through the fog of Yuuki's thoughts, but it usually left him feeling like he'd survived a typhoon—drenched and with the bridges he built washed away.

"Mom wants grandchildren…"

Miko's piercing stare called bullshit. "Every time you come

here it's something new. I'm going to date. I'm getting married. Never mind, I changed my mind. I need to get some woman pregnant to make my mother happy. Fuck your mother."

"But who knows how much longer she's going to be around? Why not make her happy while I can?"

"She wouldn't be happy if she found out you were miserable." Miko leaned back, letting out a long stream of smoke. "But that's not why you're upset."

The breath caught in Yuuki's throat. His muscles tensed, but everything inside told him just to say it. It would be the same problem he had for years.

"I really loved the person I was dating, but then they couldn't handle all the yakuza stuff."

"You barely do anything."

"I know."

"What did you say to them?"

Yuuki shrugged. "I just walked away."

"You need to have the courage to be bold and fight for what you want. You're a yakuza. Stop worrying about the rules."

Yuuki rubbed his thumb against his palm trying to quiet the howl in his heart. Each day had been harder than the last. He would've taken the numbness before he'd been with Kazuki over the constant lament that now plagued his broken heart.

Miko tapped the ash off her cigarette. "If you really love him, you have to be bold and fight."

Yuuki's mouth fell open. "How did you know?"

"I had my suspicions."

"Does Mom know?"

"That's for you to tell."

Yuuki had never expected his aunt already knew about

his sexuality, and he'd always worried if he came out it would be a big issue. How Mother would react was its own burden.

Inside, his chest grew lighter. Everything felt a little easier. If there was anything Yuuki needed to fight for it was Kazuki.

"Thank you," Yuuki said.

He gave his aunt a hug goodbye and was escorted from the prison by the guard outside. With each step, his confidence built along with a plan to fight for Kazuki.

Yuuki got into the car's driver seat with Jun waiting in the back.

"How did it go?" Jun asked.

"Miko agreed to the demands of the alliance," Yuuki said.

"Good." Jun nodded. "Get started with the hotel—"

"But I can't make it to the final sake exchange."

Jun's eyes narrowed. "Why? Does Miko not want you there?"

"I have plans that day. I'll pass all the information on to Father Murata's secretary. He'll handle the hotel reservations. If he can handle the boss, he can handle anything."

Jun's eyebrows drew in but loosened a moment later. "Okay. I'll make it work."

Yuuki only hoped talking to his mother and Kazuki would go as easily.

# chapter 20

*February 11*

Kazuki would sleep tomorrow.

Until then, it would be a rush of hurry up and wait. Hurrying the models to get their makeup and hair done, hurrying them into their garments, then waiting for their turn to do a quick runway practice and eventually the show. His nerves were always sparked when he had helped Hana while they'd been married, but doing all the preshow preparations solo made him feel like he was falling into an abyss.

In ten hours, he would discover if his plan to appeal to new clients would work. If he hadn't been so exhausted from the sleepless night, last-minute garment fixes, and the five a.m. wake-up call, he'd be vomiting. He rubbed his eyes and rested his hand on his stomach.

He walked to the end of the runway and jumped down to the floor while Hana waited in the wings. Employees dressed in black set up chairs alongside the side.

"Ready!" Kazuki called.

Hana motioned for the models to start, then scurried down to the floor as the music played. The sweeping strings of a traditional shamisen danced together with a modern electric guitar.

The twelve models strutted down the runway. The bright florals of the suits evoked spring. Kazuki smiled, but after a few models passed, his smile faded. Each of the model's faces turned into Yuuki's, no matter how different they looked.

Kazuki pressed his lips together, doubting he'd ever fill the void.

"We should switch two and five. It makes the transition to the red more shocking," Hana suggested.

"Sounds good," Kazuki said. "And maybe walk with a little less harshness."

"They look harsh to you?"

"Yeah, like they're going to demand some protection money."

"In those florals?" Hana laughed.

Kazuki rubbed his neck. "They don't look harsh to you?"

"You'd rather they smile?"

"That's a bit extreme. Maybe if they thought less CEO doubling profits and more stylish dad getting ice cream with the kids."

"They have to be the CEO to afford the suits."

The stage manager signaled that their time was up. Hana and Kazuki walked backstage and wrangled their models to their designated waiting area.

"I lost a button." One of the models pointed to the thread hanging from his jacket.

"How could you lose a button?" Kazuki said. "You've been wearing that suit for less than ten minutes."

The model shrugged.

A dull buzz sprung up in the space between Kazuki's eyes. He patted his pockets for a needle and thread.

"I've got it," Hana said. "Hand over your coat."

Hana pulled out a sewing bag and began threading a needle.

Kazuki rubbed his head. "I can't believe I forgot to bring a sewing kit."

"It's your first show."

"I helped with your shows for years."

Hana waved her hand. "That's different."

"Let me sew the button on so you can get back to your own designs."

"I have one of the assistant designers dealing with them. She's happy to show me what she can do."

"You're not having your new husband do it?"

"He's at home with the baby."

"Oh, I thought they'd at least come to the show."

"I wanted to be for myself for a bit." Hana's smile put Kazuki at ease.

"That's understandable. I was hoping to see your daughter again."

"You could always visit."

"I would feel awkward."

"None of that matters now, right? Or at least that's how I see it." She held up the coat. "There. All fixed."

She handed the coat back to the model. Her warm smile faded when she turned her attention back to Kazuki. He gulped. She tilted her head, and Kazuki had to look away from her persistent gaze. The silence pressed against the aching void in his heart.

She hooked her arm around Kazuki's and pulled him away from the models.

"What's going on?" she asked. "You should be so ecstatic

you're going to rip your hair out. The garments are awesome. Everyone will love them. You know I wouldn't let you design something bad with my name attached."

"Nerves."

"You're either lying to me or yourself with that line."

"I..." Kazuki rubbed his neck. "I'm fine."

"I was married to you for too long not to be able to tell when something is wrong."

Kazuki hoped he could hide his feelings from himself, but he could never hide them from Hana. Perhaps without the fog of insomnia, he could have put on a better act. But he hurt, a screaming, stomping kind of hurt. A hurt that clouded his thoughts with static.

"It's the suits," Kazuki said, shocked he could even begin to speak what his heart whispered to him.

"What about them? I have enough buttons to fix them all."

"They remind me of Yuuki."

"And that makes you sad because?"

"We broke up." Kazuki swallowed. "I broke up with him."

"You sounded so happy when you talked about him."

"He's a yakuza." Kazuki covered his face with his hands.

"And?"

"And? He's in the mob!"

"The Kyoto mob is different, more traditional. Many yakuza have wives. They make it work. You two could do the same."

"Not when every time he gets a call, I'm worried he'll have to leave, and he won't come back because he'll be dead." The words leapt out of Kazuki's heart and once they were finally in the air, a vacuum swallowed him whole.

"You always focused on the negative things," Hana said.

"How can you blame me with everything going on? You've

seen the news. Think of all the things *not* being reported because they're being covered up."

"That's why you should focus on the moments you have together, not on what might happen. It's like if I knew we would get divorced going into the marriage, how could I ever have enjoyed the good times?"

Hana's words hit Kazuki like a bullet.

"Like family members of firefighters or the self-defense force," Kazuki said. "Their family can't worry that they won't be home for dinner each night."

"Exactly," Hana said. "Now when are you going to call and apologize so you can enjoy your debut?"

Kazuki laughed and pulled out his phone. He stared at it. He wanted to call Yuuki to get the buzz out from under his skin.

But Yuuki was working.

It would've been the easy thing for him to call and disrupt Yuuki's work. But Kazuki had to wait and for once put someone before himself.

"I'll do it after the show. I couldn't take it if he turned me down again."

# chapter 11

Yuuki stood in his mother's kitchen as she scurried about preparing lunch. The dogs wove between his legs. Two of the pack of Pomeranians stood on their hind legs, begging for food.

Yuuki opened his mouth, then closed it again. His stomach leapt into his throat each time he tried to speak.

"Go ahead and relax," Mom said. "I don't need help making lunch."

"I don't need lunch," Yuuki said.

"What kind of mother would I be if I didn't offer lunch to my son?"

Miko's words echoed in Yuuki's mind like they had the past week. It would've been easier for Yuuki to go along with his mother's wishes, but it wouldn't do him any good.

Yuuki swallowed, but his mouth stayed dry. "There's something I have to tell you."

"I'll make sure to roast the sesame seeds how you like."

"Not that."

"Oh?"

Finally, she stopped washing the rice and turned to look

at him. Yuuki couldn't tell if the glint in her eyes was worry or anticipation.

"I found someone I really care about," Yuuki said. "They make me happy."

"That's good news."

"But I'm not the marrying type, and I don't want children. I should've told you sooner."

Yuuki closed his eyes.

Waiting for her tears.

Waiting for her screams.

But only the hissing sound of the rice cooker came.

"Why do you think I would be upset?" she asked.

"Because every time I'm here, you talk about wanting grandchildren."

"I talk about it because I don't want you to be lonely when I'm gone." She laughed and hugged Yuuki. "I just want you to be happy."

Yuuki took in the first deep lungful of air he could remember. Mom squeezed him tighter than he believed she could.

"When do I get to meet him?" she asked.

"W-what?" Yuuki's words shook.

Mom smiled and gave Yuuki's shoulder a light squeeze. "When you're ready, I want to meet him. This person who makes you happy."

Yuuki's legs shook. His whole world had titled, but instead of knocking him off-balance, it caused everything to finally click into alignment.

He pressed his lips together, unable to find any other words but, "Thanks, Mom."

"Now, go rest and let me finish lunch so we can chat."

"Actually, I have a show I need to get to, but I'll call you tomorrow to set up a real lunch." Yuuki's cheeks grew hot. "If I'm lucky, then I'll bring him."

Mom said a heartfelt goodbye, and Yuuki left for Kazuki's fashion show. He stopped by the florist to pick up a large bouquet first.

The line outside the building moved along at a steady pace. Every person handed the attendant an invitation card before gaining entry. Yuuki waited in line even though he hadn't received an invitation.

The scent of roses filled his nose, but it only made his heart beat faster. He was a yakuza. He wasn't going to let something like the lack of an invitation stop him.

"Invitation?" the attendant asked.

Yuuki held up the bouquet. "Delivery."

"Deliveries are in the back. Leave them on the table."

Yuuki followed where the attendant pointed and headed to the back of the building. Instead of the orderly line like the one out front, the back was chaos. Real plant and flower delivery people dashed here and there, trying to get people to sign for things before dropping them off at a table next to the door. Luckily, a group of smokers had propped the back door open with a brick, and Yuuki slipped inside.

If the outside was chaotic, then the inside was sheer pandemonium. The shuffling of people dashing this way and that and the collective volume of so many people speaking was overwhelming.

He walked past the line of makeup artists to a cluster of models wearing Kazuki's floral suits.

"Yuuki? What are you doing here?" Kazuki asked, his tone more surprised than angry. At least he wasn't screaming.

"I wanted to give you these." Yuuki held out the bouquet. "Congratulations on the show."

Kazuki didn't take the flowers, but their gazes met, and

the pandemonium around them faded. Kazuki's eyes glistened, and Yuuki fought the urge to reach out and hold him.

"You're supposed to be in Hokkaido," Kazuki said.

"I told my boss I had more important things to do. I wanted to be here with you."

Kazuki embraced Yuuki. He dropped the flowers and leaned deeper into Kazuki's warmth.

"I shouldn't have walked away before," Yuuki whispered into Kazuki's ear. "I don't want to let you go again."

"I don't either. I know there are parts of your life you can't control, and no one can ever know what tomorrow brings."

"Hopefully, my tomorrow includes you."

Kazuki smiled. "It does, and I'll cherish every moment we have together."

If they had been anywhere else, Yuuki wouldn't have pulled Kazuki into a deep kiss, but with the flurry of people around them, Yuuki doubted anyone would notice.

"Okamoto and Akamatsu collaboration up next!" a voice called over the microphone.

Kazuki squeezed Yuuki's hand. "Watch the show with me."

Hand and hand they walked to the curtain. The way they should've been from the beginning.


*1 Month Later…*


Yuuki broke the doggie treat into pieces and offered one to each of his mother's dogs along with a handshake. She hadn't gotten another one… yet.

"Kazuki will be able to make it for dinner next week," Yuuki said. "He's been training a new front clerk, so he can't do this week."

"What are some of his favorite foods? I'll cook them when he's here."

"You don't need to prepare anything special."

"It's good to make a good impression."

Yuuki laughed. "You met him already. Years ago. And again on the sidewalk that one night."

Mom waved her hand. "It's different now."

"Well, don't overthink it. I gotta get going. We'll see you next week."

"Before you go, I have something for you. Let me go get it."

She disappeared into her bedroom. The pack of dogs followed behind her. Yuuki swore he heard a meow, but he must've been hearing things.

"I don't need anything, Mom," Yuuki called.

"Don't worry. I saw her and thought of you."

"Her?"

The dogs turned the corner first, their tails wagging. Mom had something in her hands. Small, pink, and resembling a rat? Yuuki narrowed his eyes. That couldn't be right.

"She's for you." Mom held out her hands to reveal a tiny hairless kitten. It was wearing a tiny blue-and-red knitted shirt.

"You got me a kitten?" he said.

"Yes, she's my grandkitten. Isn't the little shirt cute? I thought about making her a hat next."

She put the kitten in Yuuki's hands. The cat let out a tiny meow that melted the last big chunk of Yuuki's resistance.

"But why a cat and not a dog?" Yuuki asked.

"Walking a dog takes time, and you're busy with work. Also, your aunt mentioned how your boss had a hairless cat, and I kept thinking about it, and it seemed perfect. Isn't she cute?"

"She so tiny I could carry her in my pocket."

"Well, she was the runt."

Yuuki held up the cat in one hand, her yellow eyes meeting his. "I can see."

—

Yuuki rubbed the kitten's head and slipped her into his coat pocket. He opened the door to Kazuki's apartment.

"Welcome home," Kazuki called from the kitchen. "I figured we could try cooking eel again."

"Hopefully there'll be less smoke this time."

Kazuki laughed and tied his hair up. "I think I figured out the oil temperature this time."

"We have a kid now."

"What?"

Yuuki pulled the kitten from his pocket. She sniffed the ground before scampering around and pawing at Kazuki's house slipper. Kazuki's face glowed with a smile.

"She's so adorable!" he said.

"My mom said she's her grandkitten."

"I was hoping she could stay at your house since your schedule is pretty set." Yuuki cracked a smile. "You won't even have to worry about cat hair."

"Of course, little Cookie can stay here," Kazuki said.

"We're not calling her Cookie."

"Muffin?"

"No food. Mom has enough food dog names for me."

"Okay, we'll think of something, but it has to be cute to match her." Kazuki scooped up the cat and gave her a snuggle. "Oh, I finished tailoring your suit jackets."

"I can't believe they bugged you so much that you took in all of them."

"I cringe every time you wear something I didn't make. You should be happy I didn't give you a new wardrobe. Here. I want you to try one on."

Kazuki carried the kitten to the bedroom, put her on the bed, and gave Yuuki a suit. Yuuki slipped it on. He could admit how nice the adjustments Kazuki had made to his suits made them feel.

"You like it?" Kazuki asked.

"Yeah, it's nice. The sleeves are much better."

"Look in the pocket."

Yuuki opened the pocket but saw nothing but some extra stitching.

"*Inside* the pocket," Kazuki repeated.

Even upside down, Yuuki recognized the characters. "It's your name."

Kazuki nodded, a few strands of hair falling into his face. He pressed his hand to Yuuki's chest. "This way, no matter where you are, I'm always over your heart."

Their lips brushed together in a kiss, but before Yuuki could deepen it, the cat meowed. They both looked at her. She seemed very upset at the lack of attention.

"We should probably go get some food and a litter box for our kitten," Yuuki said.

Kazuki shook his head. "It'll be late when we get back, so we might as well go to the eel house for dinner."

Yuuki laughed. "Sure, we can spoil our kitten, then spoil ourselves."

# Author note

Thank you so much for reading! I admit, this book took much longer than I intended. A lot went on during the writing of this novel. I got a promotion at work, completely burned out, quit, learned a bunch of new of skills, and finally got a new job!

My previous book, *Addicted to Lust*, came out a few days after the burn-me-out-in-no-time promotion. I remember being so stressed out that I thought I'd never publish another book again. I'm glad that proved false. The completion of *My Heart's Desire* feels like such a triumph. And it is.

A lot of my job stress bled into this story. There were a lot of moments where I was rooting Fujio and countless pages of side plot about Kazuki's hiring process that ended up getting cut—which was for the best. I enjoyed getting to spend a bit more time with Yuuki since he had such minor appearances in the main Yakuza Path series. I purposely wanted to write more women characters in this book. I wanted them to be the characters with all the right answers and the clearest heads on their shoulders while the guys were hopeless.

So thank you, with all my heart, for reading. I would be enterally grateful if you would write a review or recommend this book to a friend. If enough people read my novels, then I won't have to worry about a day job at all!

Thanks so much for your continued support,
Amy
January 2023

# What to read next?

If you like your yakuza stories with a lot more blood, gore, and death, then I recommend the Yakuza Path series. *Blood Stained Tea*, the first book in the series, is free. Grab it as your next read. If you want some more yakuza action where Yuuki and Kazuki make a small appearance, start with *Wrapped in Screams*. (Be warned that the Yakuza Path series is not for the faint of heart)

If you enjoy blood-free reads and already read *Addicted to Lust*, check out the Would it be Okay to Love You? series. The first book is free, and a preview of the first chapter can be found at the end of this book.

# THE YAKUZA PATH UNIVERSE READING ORDER
(as of 2023)

*The Yakuza Path: Blood Stained Tea*

*The Yakuza Path: Better Than Suicide*

*My Heart's Desire (A Yakuza Path Romance)*

*The Yakuza Path: One Thousand Cranes*

*Addicted to Lust (A Yakuza Path Romance)*

*The Yakuza Path: The Deafening Silence*

*The Yakuza Path: Flowers of Flesh and Blood*

*The Yakuza Path: Wrapped in Screams*

Want to be some of the first to read Amy's next book?
Sign up to Amy's newsletter to get a new chapter every
month in your in box.
www.amytasukada.com/free-stuff

# CHAPTER 1

Sato planted himself in the middle of the do-it-your-self Gundam robot model kits. He could rattle off the names of each robot figure with a single glance and could whip up an Excel presentation about the anime series within minutes. But today he frowned because the bright-colored boxes offered nothing new.

He pushed up his dark-rimmed glasses with a sigh and moved along the aisle. With the three-day vacation, he needed something to occupy his time besides binge-watching old anime DVDs and eating vending machine snacks.

Sato jerked as he bumped into a teenager who apparently shared his love of model kits.

"Sorry." He took a step back. "I didn't see you there."

The teenager waved off the apology with a smile. He had to be the shortest person Sato had ever seen outside of primary school, but Sato loomed over everyone he met, so he wasn't the right person to judge. Sato had started assembling the kits when he was around the teen's age, which probably added to his having trouble finding a new one. Smiling back, Sato resumed his search.

The first soft strings of Beethoven's Ninth Symphony played over the anime shop's speakers. Even in Sato's favorite store he couldn't escape the holiday song.

"I can't believe they're playing this song here," the teen said. "I'll be glad when the New Year's over so I don't have to hear it for another eleven months."

A fit of giggles erupted from the checkout line, cutting

off any reply Sato would've given—not that he'd planned on giving one to the teen.

Sato peeked over the robot display and caught a look at the group of laughing women. They all clutched the same CD. No major anime soundtracks had dropped today, but Sato only kept track of Gundam releases or the series he did the accounting for. It was probably for some magical girl anime release.

He ignored their laughter from there and went back to searching for kits. He had New Year's money to spend.

After a few more minutes of searching, Sato found two model kits worthy of assembling. He liked one figure more, but the other would be more challenging. After all, he couldn't spend his entire New Year's vacation watching anime like last year.

"It's really hard to pick one sometimes, isn't it?" Sato said.

"I guess so," the teenager said.

Sato bit his lip. Usually he wouldn't hold a conversation with random strangers, but the teen clearly loved Gundam as much as he did. Why else would he linger as much as he had?

The teenager lifted his sunglasses and perched them on his black beanie. Blond hair peeked out from under the hat. He smiled at Sato, showing the dimples on his cheeks.

"They let you dye your hair in school now?" Sato blurted out without thinking. "A friend of mine got in trouble when he lightened his to brown."

"I'm twenty-five."

"Oh, please excuse me, I didn't mean…" Sato bit his lip.

"Is it because I'm short?" The dimples disappeared, and a mischievous glint appeared in the man's green eyes. "Maybe you're just really tall."

"Sorry."

"Don't worry so much. I once bought my friend a pack of

cigarettes and a cop popped out of nowhere and said I was too young to use the vending machine. He went into this big lecture, then I showed him my ID and he thought it was a fake! He threatened to call my parents and everything."

Sato gave a weary smile and rubbed the back of his neck. Knowing the blond was close to his own age zapped away what little social courage he possessed.

The man's gaze met Sato's, then wandered down his body without shame. Sato's face grew hot, and his heart thumped in his ears.

"So is everything else about you as big?" he asked.

"I—ah…"

The guy was actually flirting with him? Sato's technique consisted of vaguely making eye contact and hoping the other person realized he was into him. The way the blond's crooked smile spread across his face didn't make Sato's heart beat any quieter.

In the accounting department, the most out-there anyone got was wearing a khaki suit. Sato had never even talked to anyone bold enough to wear colored contacts and dye their hair so drastically. He pushed up his glasses but couldn't squeak out a reply.

"So which one did you decide on getting?" the blond asked.

Sato swallowed. The man still wanted to hold a conversation with him?

"I think this one." Sato picked a five-hour do-it-yourself kit. It would take him three if he was lucky.

"Nice choice."

Sato rubbed his sweaty palms against his coat. "I—ah— which one are you getting?"

"Oh, these."

He held up a few manga graphic novels. The cover of one

had a man clinging onto another man, his private parts covered by a conveniently placed bedsheet. They were boys' love novels. Sato's tongue twisted into a Windsor knot like his tie.

If the guy was reading them, then he surely had to be gay, or at least bi. Though the fact he'd flirted with Sato had to be the biggest giveaway.

Sato's breath caught in his throat even thinking of buying a gay manga himself.

Sure he'd dated people who were out before. There'd been that upperclassman in high school, but that had only lasted three days. His college boyfriend had lasted longer. They'd been in the same trigonometry class and had even studied together. Then he'd stopped taking Sato's calls after the final exam. Sato tugged at his tie. He couldn't really count those as meaningful relationships.

The man stared at Sato.

"So you're not getting a kit?" Sato asked.

"I ducked here to hide from them." The blond pointed to the door where the group of women walked out.

"All of them?"

He laughed. "What can I say?"

Heading to the boys' love section with a gaggle of boyX-boy-crazed women would have any man running to avoid their questions. The blond was cute, too, so they probably would've wanted to snap a photo.

"Well, ah—" Sato cleared his throat. "Nice talking to you."

Sato knew when he was defeated and walked to the checkout line. The blond was so different from the guys at the accounting office that Sato couldn't carry on any more of a conversation. His words tangled in his mouth like adding-machine paper on tax day.

Sato rubbed the corner of the cardboard box. Once he cracked it open, he'd forget all about the man.

The last woman left, and only nerds like Sato were left in line. Outside of events, the anime store rarely got busy, but with New Year's everyone had extra cash to spend.

The blond got in line behind him, and the ball of nerves in Sato twisted tighter. Normal people could have conversations with people who flirted with them, but all Sato could do was gnaw on his bottom lip and look like the biggest loser ever. No wonder his Gundam robot collection outnumbered the people he interacted with. He'd seem like a bigger idiot if he didn't at least attempt to say something… anything.

The music switched to an anime theme that Sato recognized. It wasn't something he really watched, but it was popular.

"This anime is everywhere," Sato pushed out. "Almost as bad as the Ninth Symphony and New Year's."

"That's for sure." The blond laughed, and it lit up Sato's world.

"Have you listened to the soundtrack for the *Mobile Suit Gundam*? That's my favorite of all of them."

It was a classic.

"I admit I've never watched anything Gundam."

How could anyone not watch Gundam? Sato cocked an eyebrow. "Really? None at all?"

"Parents wouldn't let me watch TV."

Not being able to talk about robots killed most of the topics Sato could talk about.

"What soundtracks do you like, then?" Sato asked.

"If I had to choose, there's an anime called *Gravitation*. I liked that soundtrack," the blond said. "Maybe more how they put the album together than the songs themselves."

"Oh, I've never heard of it."

"It was about this rock star and a writer and their relationship. They had a real musician sing all the songs, so it was fun. They didn't really match the voices that well, though."

"The voices didn't match?"

"The singer had a distinct singing voice so when the voice actor was acting his lines it was a little hard to believe they were the same person. They tried, but you could tell."

Sato shrugged. "I guess they should've had the singer say the character lines."

"Then you end up with someone who can't really act. Like when they get athletes to play roles in movies."

They moved up in line, and the blond pointed to a CD by the checkout. "That one's pretty good."

It had two guys on the cover and looked like one of those slow coming-of-age stories. They always had relaxing soundtracks, so it could make for something good to listen to while he assembled the robot.

Sato reached the counter and placed the CD on top of the model kit.

"I hope you like it." The blond winked.

The store clerk rang up Sato's purchases; then Sato nodded a goodbye to the blond and walked out.

The cold chill hit his face, and a light dusting of snow floated down from the sky before disappearing as it hit the ground. Sato headed home, but with each step he took his thoughts remained on the guy he'd left behind. He had to at least know his name.

Sato stopped.

He'd never been so curious about someone in his life. Maybe he could ask him more about the soundtrack, then slip in the name question. If his tongue didn't get tied into a dozen knots first.

The blond walked out of the store, his sunglasses pulled over his green eyes. He stuffed his hands into the pockets of his jacket, that looked way too thin for the Tokyo winter. The guy was so tiny he had to be freezing. His butt did look really nice in those jeans, though.

"Wait," Sato called, coming to his senses.

With Sato's long legs, he caught up with the man quickly.

"Hey, we just met at the anime store," Sato said. "I—I guess you remember, since it just happened."

Could he be any lamer?

"What's up, big boy?"

Sato cleared his throat. "What I mean to say is—ah. What's your name?"

The man raised an eyebrow. "Only my name?"

"If that's okay? I know we just met and you're not into Gundam—"

"Aoi," he interrupted. "My name is Aoi."

Sato blinked. The man gave his first name. It was way too informal for just meeting.

"I mean, what's your surname?"

"It's just Aoi."

"Well, Aoi." Sato's cheeks grew hot. "You can call me Sato."

"Nice to meet you, Sato. I hope for your favor in the coming year."

The mix of informality with Sato being able to say Aoi's first name and then the formal happy New Year's wish threw Sato off so much that he missed Aoi walking off. Sato already looked like a fool; there was no reason to make it worse by looking like a creepy stalker.

Sato sighed. It wasn't like Aoi would be the kind of guy that would want to hang out with him anyway. At least he had the model to get his mind off what a failure he was at picking up guys.

Read the rest of the romantic story for free today!
books2read.com/would1

# about the author

Amy Tasukada lives in North Texas with a calico cat called O'Hara. As an only child her day dreams kept her entertained, and at the age of ten she started to put them to paper. Since then her love of writing hasn't ceased. When she is not penning her next book she can be found drinking tea in a frilly dress.

Amy Tasukada loves hearing from her readers. You can contact her through her website, and also find out how to be first to read her next book!

Website: www.amytasukada.com

www.ingramcontent.com/pod-product-compliance
Lightning Source LLC
Chambersburg PA
CBHW061450210726
48287CB00007B/2446